"I hit him, I hit him!
'Tis a stag of ten branches, and I hit him."

THE LITTLE DUKE

BY

CHARLOTTE M. YONGE

ILLUSTRATED BY

GEORGE LAWSON

THE SAALFIELD PUBLISHING COMPANY
AKRON, OHIO   NEW YORK
MADE IN U. S. A.

FULL-PAGE ILLUSTRATIONS

THE LITTLE DUKE

CHAPTER I

On a bright autumn day, as long ago as the year 943, there was a great bustle in the Castle of Bayeux in Normandy.

The hall was large and low, the roof arched, and supported on thick short columns, almost like the crypt of a cathedral; the walls were thick, and the windows, which had no glass, were very small, set in such a depth of wall that there was a wide deep window seat, upon which the rain might beat without reaching the interior of the room. And even if it had come in, there was nothing for it to hurt, for the walls were of rough stone and the floor of tiles. There was a fire at each end of this great dark apartment, but there were no chimneys over the ample hearths, and the smoke curled about in thick white folds in the vaulted roof, adding to the wreaths of soot, which made the hall look still darker.

The fire at the lower end was by far the largest and hottest. Great black cauldrons hung over it, and servants, both men and women, with red faces, bare and grimed arms, and long iron hooks, or pots and pans, were busied around it. At the other end, which was raised about three steps above the floor of the hall, other servants were engaged. Two young maidens were strewing fresh rushes on the floor; some men were setting up a long table of rough boards, supported on trestles, and then ranging upon it silver cups, drinking horns, and wooden trenchers.

Benches were placed to receive most of the guests, but in the middle, at the place of honour, was a high chair with very thick crossing legs, and the arms curiously carved with lions' faces and claws; a clumsy wooden footstool was set in front, and the silver drinking-cup on the table was of far more beautiful workmanship than the others, richly chased with vine leaves and grapes, and figures of little boys with goats' legs. If that cup could have told its story, it would have been a strange one, for it had been made long since, in the old Roman times, and been carried off from Italy by some Northman pirate.

From one of these scenes of activity to the other, there moved a stately old lady: her long thick light hair, hardly touched with grey, was bound round her head, under a tall white cap, with a band passing under her chin; she wore a long sweeping dark robe, with wide hanging sleeves, and thick gold earrings and necklace, which had possibly come from the same quarter as the cup. She directed the servants, inspected both the cookery and arrangements of the table, held council with an old steward, now and then looked rather anxiously from the window, as if expecting some one, and began to say something about fears that these loitering youths would not bring home the venison in time for Duke William's supper.

Presently she looked up rejoiced, for a few notes of a bugle-horn were sounded; there was a clattering of feet, and in a few moments there bounded into the hall a boy about eight years old, his cheeks and large blue eyes bright with air and exercise, and his long light-brown hair streaming behind him as he ran forward flourishing a bow in his hand, and crying out, "I hit him, I hit him! Dame Astrida, do you hear? 'Tis a stag of ten branches, and I hit him in the neck."

"You! my Lord Richard! you killed him?"

"Oh no, I only struck him. It was Osmond's shaft that took him in the eye, and— Look you, Fru Astrida, he came thus through the wood, and I stood here, it might be, under the great elm, with my bow thus—" And Richard was beginning to act over again the whole scene of the deer-hunt, but Fru, that is to say Lady, Astrida, was too busy to listen, and broke in with, "Have they brought home the haunch?"

"Yes, Walter is bringing it. I had a long arrow——"

A stout forester was at this instant seen bringing in the venison, and Dame Astrida hastened to meet it, and give directions, little Richard following her all the way, and talking as eagerly as if she was attending to him—showing how he shot, how Osmond shot, how the deer bounded, and how it fell, and then counting the branches of its antlers, always ending with, "This is something to tell my father. Do you think he will come soon?"

In the meantime two men entered the hall, one about fifty, the other, one- or two-and-twenty, both in hunting dresses of plain leather, crossed by broad embroidered belts supporting a knife and a bugle-horn. The elder was broad-shouldered, sunburnt, ruddy, and rather stern-looking; the younger, who was also the taller, was slightly made, and very active, with a bright keen grey eye and merry smile. These were Dame Astrida's son, Sir Eric de Centeville, and her grandson, Osmond; and to their care Duke William of Normandy had committed his only child, Richard, to be fostered, or brought up.

It was always the custom among the Northmen that young princes should thus be put under the care of some trusty vassal instead of being brought up at home, and one reason why the Centevilles had been chosen by Duke William was that both Sir Eric and his mother spoke only the old Norwegian tongue, which he wished young Richard to understand well, whereas, in other parts of the duchy, the Normans had forgotten their own tongue, and had taken up what was then called the *Langué d'oui,* a language between German and Latin, which was the beginning of French.

On this day Duke William himself was expected at Bayeux, to pay a visit to his son before setting out on a journey to settle the disputes between the Counts of Flanders and Montreuil, and this was the reason of Fru Astrida's great preparations. No sooner had she seen the haunch placed upon a spit, which a little boy was to turn before the fire, than she turned to dress something else, namely, the young Prince Richard himself, whom she led off to one of the upper rooms, and there he had full time to talk, while she, great lady though she was, herself combed smooth his long flowing curls, and fastened his short scarlet cloth tunic, which just reached to his knee, leaving his neck, arms, and legs bare. He begged hard to be allowed to wear a short, beautifully ornamented dagger at his belt, but this Fru Astrida would not allow.

"You will have enough to do with steel and dagger before your life is at an end," said she, "without seeking to begin over soon."

"To be sure I shall," answered Richard. "I will be called Richard of the Sharp Axe, or the Bold Spirit, I promise you, Fru Astrida. We are as brave in these days as the Sigurds and Ragnars you sing of! I only wish there were serpents and dragons to slay here in Normandy."

"Never fear but you will find even too many of them," said Dame Astrida; "there be dragons of wrong here and everywhere, quite as venomous as any in my Sagas."

"I fear them not," said Richard, but half understanding her, "if you would only let me have the dagger! But, hark! hark!"—he darted to the window—"They come, they come! There is the banner of Normandy."

2

Away ran the happy child, and never rested
till he stood at the bottom of the long, steep,
stone stair leading to the embattled porch.
Thither came the Baron de Centeville and his
son, to receive their Prince. Richard looked
up at Osmond, saying, "Let me hold his stirrup," and then sprang up and shouted for joy,
as under the arched gateway there came a
tall black horse bearing the stately form of the
Duke of Normandy. His purple robe was fastened round him by a rich belt, sustaining the
mighty weapon from which he was called
"William of the Long Sword"; his legs and
feet were cased in linked steel chainwork, his
gilded spurs were on his heels, and his short
brown hair was covered by his ducal cap of
purple, turned up with fur, and a feather
fastened in by a jewelled clasp. His brow was
grave and thoughtful, and there was something both of dignity and sorrow in his face,
at the first moment of looking at it, recalling
the recollection that he had early lost his
young wife, the Duchess Emma, and that he
was beset by many cares and toils; but the

next glance generally conveyed encouragement, so full of mildness were his eyes, and
so kind the expression of his lips.

And now, how bright a smile beamed upon
the little Richard, who, for the first time, paid
him the duty of a pupil in chivalry, by holding
the stirrup while he sprang from his horse.
Next, Richard knelt to receive his blessing,
which was always the custom when children
met their parents. The Duke laid his hand on
his head, saying, "God of His mercy bless thee,
my son," and lifting him in his arms, held him
to his breast, and let him cling to his neck and
kiss him again and again before setting him
down, while Sir Eric came forward, bent his
knee, kissed the hand of his Prince, and wel-
comed him to his castle.

It would take too long to tell all the friendly
and courteous words that were spoken, the
greeting of the Duke and the noble old Lady
Astrida, and the reception of the barons who
had come in the train of their lord. Richard
was bidden to greet them, but, though he held
out his hand as desired, he shrank a little to

his father's side, gazing at them in dread and shyness.

There was Count Bernard, of Harcourt, called "the Dane,"[1] with his shaggy red hair and beard, to which a touch of grey had given a strange unnatural tint, his eyes looking fierce and wild under his thick eyebrows, one of them misshapen in consequence of a sword cut, which had left a broad red and purple scar across both cheek and forehead. There, too, came tall Baron Rainulf, of Ferrières, cased in a linked steel hauberk, that rang as he walked, and the men-at-arms, with helmets and shields, looking as if Sir Eric's armour that hung in the hall had come to life and was walking about.

They sat down to Fru Astrida's banquet, the old lady at the Duke's right hand, and the Count of Harcourt on his left. Osmond carved for the Duke, and Richard handed his cup and trencher. All through the meal the Duke and his lords talked earnestly of the expedition on

[1] Bernard was founder of the family of Harcourt of Nuneham; Ferrières, the ancestor of that of Ferrars.

which they were bound, to meet Count Arnulf of Flanders, on a little islet in the river Somme, there to come to some agreement by which Arnulf might make restitution to Count Herluin of Montreuil for certain wrongs which he had done him.

Some said that this would be the fittest time for requiring Arnulf to yield up some towns on his borders to which Normandy had long laid claim; but the Duke shook his head, saying that he must seek no selfish advantage when called to judge between others.

Richard was rather tired of their grave talk, and thought the supper very long; but at last it was over; the grace was said, the boards which had served for tables were removed, and, as it was still light, some of the guests went to see how their steeds had been bestowed, others to look at Sir Eric's horses and hounds, and others collected together in groups.

The Duke had time to attend to his little boy, and Richard sat upon his knee and talked; told about all his pleasures—how his arrow had hit the deer to-day, how Sir Eric let him ride out to the chase on his little pony, how Osmond would take him to bathe in the cool bright river, and how he had watched the raven's nest in the top of the old tower.

Duke William listened and smiled, and seemed as well pleased to hear as the boy was to tell. "And Richard," said he at last, "have you nought to tell me of Father Lucas, and his great book? What, not a word? Look up, Richard, and tell me how it goes with the learning."

"Oh, father!" said Richard in a low voice, playing with the clasp of his father's belt, and looking down, "I don't like those crabbed letters on the old yellow parchment."

"But you try to learn them, I hope?" said the Duke.

"Yes, father, I do, but they are very hard, and the words are so long, and Father Lucas will always come when the sun is so bright, and the wood so green, that I know not how to bear to be kept poring over those black hooks and strokes!"

"Poor little fellow," said Duke William, smiling, and Richard, rather encouraged, went on more boldly, "You do not know this reading, noble father?"

"To my sorrow, no," said the Duke.

"And Sir Eric cannot read, nor Osmond, nor any one, and why must I read, and cramp my fingers with writing, just as if I was a clerk instead of a young Duke?" Richard looked up in his father's face, and then hung his head, as if half ashamed of questioning his will, but the Duke answered him without displeasure.

"It is hard, no doubt, my boy, to you now, but it will be the better for you in the end. I would give much to be able myself to read those holy books which I must now only hear read to me by a clerk; but since I have had the wish, I have had no time to learn as you have now."

"But knights and nobles never learn," said Richard.

"And do you think it a reason they never should? But you are wrong, my boy, for the Kings of France and England, the Counts of

Anjou, of Provence, and Paris, yes, even King Hako of Norway,[1] can all read. I tell you, Richard, when the treaty was drawn up for restoring this King Louis to his throne, I was ashamed to find myself one of the few crown vassals who could not write his name thereto."

"But none is so wise or so good as you, father," said Richard proudly. "Sir Eric often says so."

"Sir Eric loves his Duke too well to see his faults," said Duke William; "but far better and wiser might I have been had I been taught by such masters as you may be. And hark, Richard, not only can all Princes here read, but in England, King Ethelstane would have every noble taught; they study in his own palace with his brothers, and read the good words that King Alfred the truth-teller put into their own tongue for them."

[1] Hako of Norway was educated by Ethelstane of England. It was Foulques le bon, the contemporary Count of Anjou, who, when derided by Louis IV. for serving in the choir of Tours, wrote the following retort:—"The Count of Anjou to the King of France. Understand, Monseigneur, that a king without learning is a crowned ass."

"I hate the English," said Richard, raising his head and looking very fierce.

"Hate them? and wherefore?"

"Because they traitorously killed the brave sea-king Ragnar! Fru Astrida sings his death-song, which he chanted when the vipers were gnawing him to death, and he gloried to think how his sons would bring the ravens to feast upon the Saxon. Oh! had I been his son, how I would have carried on the feud! How I would have laughed when I cut down the false traitors, and burnt their palaces!" Richard's eye kindled, and his words, as he spoke the old Norse language, flowed into the sort of wild verse in which the Sagas, or legendary songs, were composed, and which, perhaps, he was unconsciously repeating.

Duke William looked grave.

"Fru Astrida must sing you no more such Sagas," said he, "if they fill your mind with these revengeful thoughts, fit only for the worshippers of Odin and Thor. Neither Ragnar nor his sons knew better than to rejoice in this deadly vengeance, but we, who are

Christians, know that it is for us to forgive."

"The English had slain their father!" said Richard, looking up with wondering, dissatisfied eyes.

"Yes, Richard, and I speak not against them, for they were even as we should have been, had not King Harald the Fair-haired driven your grandfather from Denmark. They had not been taught the truth, but to us it has been said, 'Forgive, and ye shall be forgiven.' Listen to me, my son; Christian as is this nation of ours, this duty of forgiveness is too often neglected, but let it not be so with you. Bear in mind, whenever you see the Cross[1] marked on our banner, or carved in stone on the churches, that it speaks of forgiveness to us; but of that pardon we shall never taste if we forgive not our enemies. Do you mark me, boy?"

Richard hesitated a little, and then said, "Yes, father, but I could never have pardoned, had I been one of Ragnar's sons."

[1] The banner of Normandy was a Cross till William the Conqueror adopted the lion.

"It may be that you will be in their case, Richard," said the Duke, "and should I fall, as it may well be I shall, in some of the contests that tear to pieces this unhappy kingdom of France, then remember what I say now. I charge you on your duty to God, and to your father, that you keep up no feud, no hatred, but rather that you should deem me best revenged when you have, with your heart and hand, given the fullest proof of forgiveness to your enemy. Give me your word that you will."

"Yes, father," said Richard, with rather a subdued tone, and resting his head on his father's shoulder. There was silence for a little space, during which he began to revive into playfulness, to stroke the Duke's short curled beard, and play with his embroidered collar.

In so doing, his fingers caught hold of a silver chain, and, pulling it out with a jerk, he saw a silver key attached to it. "Oh, what is that?" he asked eagerly. "What does that key unlock?"

"My greatest treasure," replied Duke

William, as he replaced the chain and key within his robe.

"Your greatest treasure, father! Is that your coronet?"

"You will know it one day," said his father, putting the little hand down from its too busy investigation; and some of the barons at that moment returning into the hall, he had no more leisure to bestow on his little son.

The next day, after morning service in the chapel, and breakfast in the hall, the Duke again set forward on his journey, giving Richard hopes he might return in a fortnight's time, and obtaining from him a promise that he would be very attentive to Father Lucas, and very obedient to Sir Eric de Centeville.

CHAPTER II

One evening Fru Astrida sat in her tall chair
in the chimney-corner, her distaff, with its
load of flax, in her hand, while she twisted and
drew out the thread, and her spindle danced
on the floor. Opposite to her sat, sleeping in
the chair, Sir Eric de Centeville; Osmond was
on a low bench within the chimney-corner,
trimming and shaping with his knife some
feathers of the wild goose, which were to fly
in a different fashion from their former one,
and serve, not to wing the flight of a harmless
goose, but of a sharp arrow.

The men of the household sat ranged on
benches on one side of the hall, the women on
the other; a great red fire, together with an
immense flickering lamp which hung from the
ceiling, supplied the light; the windows were
closed with wooden shutters, and the whole
apartment had a cheerful appearance. Two
or three large hounds were reposing in front

of the hearth, and among them sat little
Richard of Normandy, now smoothing down
their broad silken ears; now tickling the large
cushions of their feet with the end of one of
Osmond's feathers; now fairly pulling open
the eyes of one of the good-natured sleepy
creatures, which only stretched its legs, and
remonstrated with a sort of low groan, rather
than a growl. The boy's eyes were all the time
intently fixed on Dame Astrida, as if he would
not lose one word of the story she was telling
him—how Earl Rollo, his grandfather, had
sailed into the mouth of the Seine, and how
Archbishop Franco of Rouen had come to meet
him, and brought him the keys of the town,
and how not one Neustrian of Rouen had met
with harm from the brave Northmen. Then
she told him of his grandfather's baptism, and
how during the seven days that he wore his
white baptismal robes he had made large gifts
to all the chief churches in his dukedom of
Normandy.

"Oh, but tell of the paying homage!" said
Richard; "and how Sigurd Bloodaxe threw

down simple King Charles! Ah! how would I have laughed to see it!"

"Nay, nay, Lord Richard," said the old lady, "I love not that tale. That was ere the Norman learnt courtesy; and rudeness ought rather to be forgotten than remembered, save for the sake of amending it. No, I will rather tell you of our coming to Centeville, and how dreary I thought these smooth meads and broad soft-gliding streams compared with mine own father's fiord in Norway, shut in with the tall black rocks, and the dark pines above them, and far away the snowy mountains rising into the sky. Ah! how blue the waters were in the long summer days when I sat in my father's boat in the little fiord, and——"

Dame Astrida was interrupted. A bugle note rang out at the castle gate; the dogs started to their feet, and uttered a sudden deafening bark; Osmond sprang up, exclaiming, "Hark!" and trying to silence the hounds; and Richard, running to Sir Eric, cried, "Wake, wake, Sir Eric, my father is come! Oh haste to open the gates and admit him!"

"Peace, dogs!" said Sir Eric, slowly rising, as the blast of the horn was repeated. "Go, Osmond, with the porter, and see whether he who comes at such an hour be friend or foe. Stay you here, my lord," he added, as Richard was running after Osmond; and the little boy obeyed, and stood still, though quivering all over with impatience.

"Tidings from the Duke, I should guess," said Fru Astrida. "It can scarce be himself at such an hour."

"Oh, it must be, dear Fru Astrida!" said Richard. "He said he would come again. Hark, there are horses' feet in the court! I am sure that is his black charger's tread! And I shall not be there to hold his stirrup! Oh! Sir Eric, let me go."

Sir Eric, always a man of few words, only shook his head, and at that moment steps were heard on the stone stairs. Again Richard was about to spring forward, when Osmond returned, his face showing, at a glance, that something was amiss; but all that he said was — "Count Bernard of Harcourt and Sir

Osmond sprang up exclaiming, "Hark!"

Rainulf de Ferrières," and he stood aside to
let them pass.

Richard stood still in the midst of the hall,
disappointed. Without greeting to Sir Eric,
or to any within the hall, the Count of Harcourt came forward to Richard, bent his knee
before him, took his hand, and said with a
broken voice and heaving breast, "Richard,
Duke of Normandy, I am thy liegeman and
true vassal;" then, rising from his knees while
Rainulf de Ferrières went through the same
form, the old man covered his face with his
hands and wept aloud.

"Is it even so?" said the Baron de Centeville,
and being answered by a mournful look and
sigh from Ferrières, he too bent before the
boy, and repeated the words, "I am thy liegeman and true vassal, and swear fealty to thee
for my castle and barony of Centeville."

"Oh no, no!" cried Richard, drawing back
his hand in a sort of agony, feeling as if he was
in a frightful dream from which he could not
awake. "What means it? Oh! Fru Astrida,
tell me what means it? Where is my father?"

"Alas! my child!" said the old lady, putting her arm round him, and drawing him close to her, whilst her tears flowed fast, and Richard stood, reassured by her embrace, listening with eyes opened wide, and deep oppressed breathing, to what was passing between the four nobles, who spoke earnestly among themselves without much heed of him.

"The Duke dead!" repeated Sir Eric de Centeville, like one stunned and stupefied.

"Even so," said Rainulf, slowly and sadly, and the silence was only broken by the long-drawn sobs of old Count Bernard.

"But how? when? where?" broke forth Sir Eric presently. "There was no note of battle when you went forth. Oh, why was not I at his side?"

"He fell not in battle," gloomily replied Sir Rainulf.

"Ha! could sickness cut him down so quickly?"

"It was not sickness," answered Ferrières. "It was treachery. He fell in the isle of Pecquigny, by the hand of the false Fleming!"

"Lives the traitor yet?" cried the Baron de Centeville, grasping his good sword.

"He lives and rejoices in his crime," said Ferrières, "safe in his own merchant towns."

"I can scarce credit you, my lords!" said Sir Eric. "Our Duke slain, and his enemy safe, and you here to tell the tale!"

"I would I were stark and stiff by my lord's side!" said Count Bernard, "but for the sake of Normandy, and of that poor child, who is like to need all that ever were friends to his house. I would that mine eyes had been blinded for ever ere they had seen that sight! And not a sword lifted in his defence! Tell you how it passed, Rainulf! My tongue will not speak it."

He threw himself on a bench and covered his face with his mantle, while Rainulf de Ferrières proceeded: "You know how in an evil hour our good Duke appointed to meet this caitiff Count of Flanders in the isle of Pecquigny, the Duke and Count each bringing twelve men with them, all unarmed. Duke Alan of Brittany was one on our side, Count

Bernard here another, old Count Bothon and myself; we bore no weapon—would that we had!—but not so the false Flemings. Ah me! I shall never forget Duke William's lordly presence when he stepped ashore and doffed his bonnet to the knave Arnulf."

"Yes," interposed Bernard. "And marked you not the words of the traitor as they met? 'My lord,' quoth he, 'you are my shield and defence.' Would that I could cleave his treason-hatching skull with my battle-axe."

"So," continued Rainulf, "they conferred together, and as words cost nothing to Arnulf, he not only promised all restitution to the paltry Montreuil, but even was for offering to pay homage to our Duke for Flanders itself; but this our William refused, saying it were foul wrong to both King Louis of France, and Kaiser Otho of Germany, to take from them their vassal. They took leave of each other in all courtesy, and we embarked again. It was Duke William's pleasure to go alone in a small boat, while we twelve were together in another. Just as we had nearly reached our own bank there was a shout from the Flemings that their Count had somewhat further to say to the Duke, and, forbidding us to follow him, the Duke turned his boat and went back again. No sooner had he set foot on the isle," proceeded the Norman, clenching his hands, and speaking between his teeth, "than we saw one Fleming strike him on the head with an oar; he fell senseless, the rest threw themselves upon him, and the next moment held up their bloody daggers in scorn at us! You may well think how we shouted and yelled at them, and plied our oars like men distracted, but all in vain; they were already in their boats, and ere we could even reach the isle, they were on the other side of the river, mounted their horses, fled with coward speed, and were out of reach of a Norman's vengeance."

"But they shall not be so long!" cried Richard, starting forward; for, to his childish fancy, this dreadful history was more like one of Dame Astrida's legends than a reality, and

at the moment his thought was only of the
blackness of the treason. "Oh that I were a
man to chastise them! One day they shall
feel——"

He broke off short, for he remembered how
his father had forbidden his denunciations of
vengeance; but his words were eagerly caught
up by the barons, who, as Duke William had
said, were far from possessing any temper of
forgiveness, thought revenge a duty, and were
only glad to see a warlike spirit in their new
Prince.

"Ha! say you so, my young lord?" exclaimed
old Count Bernard, rising. "Yes, and I see a
sparkle in your eye that tells me you will one
day avenge him nobly!"

Richard drew up his head, and his heart
throbbed high as Sir Eric made answer, "Ay,
truly, that will he! You might search Normandy through, yea, and Norway likewise,
ere you would find a temper more bold and
free. Trust my word, Count Bernard, our
young Duke will be famed as widely as ever
were his forefathers!"

"I believe it well!" said Bernard. "He hath the port of his grandfather, Duke Rollo, and much, too, of his noble father! How say you, Lord Richard, will you be a valiant leader of the Norman race against our foes?"

"That I will!" said Richard, carried away by the applause excited by those few words of his. "I will ride at your head this very night if you will but go to chastise the false Flemings."

"You shall ride with us to-morrow, my lord," answered Bernard, "but it must be to Rouen, there to be invested with your ducal sword and mantle, and to receive the homage of your vassals."

Richard drooped his head without replying, for this seemed to bring to him the perception that his father was really gone, and that he should never see him again. He thought of all his projects for the day of his return, how he had almost counted the hours, and had looked forward to telling him that Father Lucas was well pleased with him! And now he should never nestle in his breast again, never hear

his voice, never see those kind eyes beam upon
him. Large tears gathered in his eyes, and
ashamed that they should be seen, he sat
down on a footstool at Fru Astrida's feet,
leant his forehead on his hands, and thought
over all that his father had done and said the
last time they were together. He fancied the
return that had been promised, going over the
meeting and the greeting, till he had almost
persuaded himself that this dreadful story
was but a dream. But when he looked up,
there were the barons, with their grave
mournful faces, speaking of the corpse, which
Duke Alan of Brittany was escorting to
Rouen, there to be buried beside the old Duke
Rollo, and the Duchess Emma, Richard's
mother. Then he lost himself in wonder how
that stiff bleeding body could be the same as
the father whose arm was so lately around
him, and whether his father's spirit knew how
he was thinking of him; and in these dreamy
thoughts the young orphan Duke of Normandy, forgotten by his vassals in their grave
councils, fell asleep, and scarce awakened

enough to attend to his prayers, when Fru
Astrida at length remembered him, and led
him away to bed.

When Richard awoke the next morning, he
could hardly believe that all that had passed
in the evening was true, but he soon found
that it was but too real, and all was prepared
for him to go to Rouen with the vassals; indeed, it was for no other purpose than to fetch
him that the Count of Harcourt had come to
Bayeux. Fru Astrida was quite unhappy that
"the child," as she called him, should go alone
with the warriors; but Sir Eric laughed at her,
and said that it would never do for the Duke
of Normandy to bring his nurse with him in
his first entry into Rouen, and she must be
content to follow at some space behind, under
the escort of Walter the Huntsman.

So she took leave of Richard, charging both
Sir Eric and Osmond to have the utmost care
of him, and shedding tears as if the parting
was to be for a much longer space; then he
bade farewell to the servants of the castle,
received the blessing of Father Lucas, and,

mounting his pony, rode off between Sir Eric and Count Bernard. Richard was but a little boy, and he did not think so much of his loss as he rode along in the free morning air, feeling himself a Prince at the head of his vassals, his banner displayed before him, and the people coming out wherever he passed to gaze on him, and call for blessings on his name. Rainulf de Ferrières carried a large heavy purse filled with silver and gold, and whenever they came to these gazing crowds Richard was well pleased to thrust his hands deep into it, and scatter handfuls of coins among the gazers, especially where he saw little children.

They stopped to dine and rest in the middle of the day at the castle of a baron, who, as soon as the meal was over, mounted his horse, and joined them in their ride to Rouen. So far it had not been very different from Richard's last journey, when he went to keep Christmas there with his father; but, now they were beginning to come nearer the town, he knew the broad river Seine again, and saw

the square tower of the Cathedral, and he remembered how at that very place his father
had met him, and how he had ridden by his
side into the town, and had been led by his
hand up to the hall.

His heart was very heavy as he recollected
there was no one now to meet and welcome
him; scarely any one to whom he could even
tell his thoughts, for those tall grave barons
had nothing to say to such a little boy, and
the very respect and formality with which
they treated him made him shrink from them
still more, especially from the grim-faced
Bernard; and Osmond, his own friend and
playfellow, was obliged to ride far behind, as
inferior in rank.

They entered the town just as it was growing dark. Count Bernard looked back and
arrayed the procession; Eric de Centeville
bade Richard sit upright and not look weary;
and then all the knights held back while the
little Duke rode alone a little in advance of
them through the gateway. There was a loud
shout of "Long live the little Duke!" and

crowds of people were standing round to gaze upon his entry, so many that the bag of coins was soon emptied by his largesses. The whole city was like one great castle, shut in by a wall and moat, and with Rollo's Tower rising at one end like the keep of a castle, and it was thither that Richard was turning his horse when the Count of Harcourt said, "Nay, my lord, to the Church of Our Lady."[1]

It was then considered a duty to be paid to the deceased that their relatives and friends should visit them as they lay in state, and sprinkle them with drops of holy water, and Richard was now to pay this token of respect. He trembled a little, and yet it did not seem quite so dreary since he should once more look on his father's face, and he accordingly rode towards the Cathedral. It was then very unlike what it is now; the walls were very thick, the windows small and almost buried in heavy carved arches; the columns within were low, clumsy, and circu-

[1] The Cathedral was afterwards built by Richard himself.

lar, and it was usually so dark that the vaulting of the roof could scarcely be seen.

Now, however, a whole flood of light poured forth from every window, and when Richard came to the door he saw not only the two tall thick candles that always burnt on each side of the altar, but in the chancel stood a double row ranged in a square, shedding a pure quiet brilliancy throughout the building, and chiefly on the silver and gold ornaments of the altar. Outside these lights knelt a row of priests in dark garments, their heads bowed over their clasped hands, and their chanted psalms sounding sweet, and full of soothing music. Within that guarded space was a bier, and a form lay on it.

Richard trembled still more with awe, and would have paused, but he was obliged to proceed. He dipped his hand in the water of the font, crossed his brow, and came slowly on, sprinkled the remaining drops on the lifeless figure, and then stood still. There was an oppression on his breast as if he could neither breathe nor move.

There lay William of the Long Sword,
like a good and true Christian warrior.

There lay William of the Long Sword, like a good and true Christian warrior, arrayed in his shining armour, his sword by his side, his shield on his arm, and a cross between his hands, clasped upon his breast. His ducal mantle of crimson velvet, lined with ermine, was round his shoulders, and instead of a helmet his coronet was on his head; but, in contrast with this rich array, over the collar of the hauberk was folded the edge of a rough hair shirt, which the Duke had worn beneath his robes, unknown to all, until his corpse was disrobed of his blood-stained garments. His face looked full of calm solemn peace, as if he had gently fallen asleep, and was only awaiting the great call to awaken. There was not a single token of violence visible about him, save that one side of his forehead bore a deep purple mark, where he had first been struck by the blow of the oar which had deprived him of sense.

"See you that, my lord?" said Count Bernard, first breaking the silence, in a low, deep, stern voice.

Richard had heard little for many hours
past save counsels against the Flemings, and
plans of bitter enmity against them; and the
sight of his murdered father, with that look
and tone of the old Dane, fired his spirit, and
breaking from his trance of silent awe and
grief, he exclaimed, "I see it, and dearly shall
the traitor Fleming abye it!" Then, encouraged by the applauding looks of the nobles,
he proceeded, feeling like one of the young
champions of Fru Astrida's songs. His cheek
was coloured, his eye lighted up, and he lifted
his head, so that the hair fell back from his
forehead; he laid his hand on the hilt of his
father's sword, and spoke on in words per-,
haps suggested by some saga. "Yes, Arnulf
of Flanders, know that Duke William of
Normandy shall not rest unavenged! On this
good sword I vow that, as soon as my arm
shall have strength——"

The rest was left unspoken, for a hand was
laid on his arm. A priest, who had hitherto
been kneeling near the head of the corpse, had
risen, and stood tall and dark over him, and,

4

looking up, he recognised the pale grave coun-
tenance of Martin, Abbot of Jumièges, his
father's chief friend and counsellor.

"Richard of Normandy, what sayest thou?"
said he sternly. "Yes, hang thy head, and reply not, rather than repeat those words. Dost
thou come here to disturb the peace of the
dead with clamours for vengeance? Dost
thou vow strife and anger on that sword
which was never drawn save in the cause of
the poor and distressed? Wouldst thou rob
Him to whose service thy life has been
pledged, and devote thyself to that of His foe?
Is this what thou hast learnt from thy blessed
father?"

Richard made no answer, but he covered
his face with his hands to hide the tears which
were fast streaming.

"Lord Abbot, Lord Abbot, this passes!"
exclaimed Bernard the Dane. "Our young
lord is no monk, and we will not see each
spark of noble and knightly spirit quenched
as soon as it shows itself."

"Count of Harcourt," said Abbot Martin,

"are these the words of a savage pagan, or of one who has been washed in yonder blessed font? Never, while I have power, shalt thou darken the child's soul with thy foul thirst of revenge, insult the presence of thy master with the crime he so abhorred, nor the temple of Him who came to pardon with thy hatred. Well do I know, ye barons of Normandy, that each drop of your blood would willingly be given, could it bring back our departed Duke, or guard his orphan child; but if ye have loved the father. do his bidding—lay aside that accursed spirit of hatred and vengeance; if ye love the child, seek not to injure his soul more deeply than even his bitterest foe, were it Arnulf himself, hath power to hurt him."

The barons were silenced whatever their thoughts might be, and Abbot Martin turned to Richard, whose tears were still dropping fast through his fingers, as the thought of those last words of his father returned more clearly upon him. The Abbot laid his hand on his head, and spoke gently to him. "These are tears of a softened heart, I trust," said he.

"I well believe that thou didst scarce know what thou wert saying."

"Forgive me!" said Richard, as well as he could speak.

"See there," said the priest, pointing to the large cross over the altar; "thou knowest the meaning of that sacred sign?"

Richard bowed his head in assent and reverence.

"It speaks of forgiveness," continued the Abbot. "And knowest thou who gave that pardon? The Son forgave His murderers; the Father them who slew His Son. And shalt thou call for vengeance?"

"But oh!" said Richard, looking up, "must that cruel murderous traitor glory unpunished in his crime, while there lies——" and again his voice was cut off by tears.

"Vengeance shall surely overtake the sinner," said Martin, "the vengeance of the Lord, and in His own good time, but it must not be of thy seeking. Nay, Richard, thou art of all men the most bound to show love and mercy to Arnulf of Flanders. Yes, when the hand of the Lord hath touched him, and bowed him down in punishment for his crime, it is then that thou, whom he hath most deeply injured, shouldest stretch out thine hand to aid him, and receive him with pardon and peace. If thou dost vow aught on the sword of thy blessed father, in the sanctuary of thy Redeemer, let it be a Christian vow."

Richard wept too bitterly to speak, and Bernard de Harcourt, taking his hand, led him away from the church.

CHAPTER III

Duke William of the Long Sword was buried the next morning in high pomp and state, with many a prayer and psalm chanted over his grave.

When this was over, little Richard, who had all the time stood or knelt nearest the corpse, in one dull heavy dream of wonder and sorrow, was led back to the palace, and there his long heavy black garments were taken off, and he was dressed in his short scarlet tunic, his hair was carefully arranged, and then he came down again into the hall, where there was a great assembly of barons, some in armour, some in long furred gowns, who had all been attending his father's burial. Richard, as he was desired by Sir Eric de Centeville, took off his cap, and bowed low in reply to the reverences with which they all greeted his entrance, and he then slowly crossed the hall, and descended the steps from the door, while they formed into a procession behind him, according to their ranks—the Duke of Brittany first, and then all the rest, down to the poorest knight who held his manor immediately from the Duke of Normandy.

Thus they proceeded, in slow and solemn order, till they came to the Church of Our Lady. The clergy were there already, ranged in ranks on each side of the choir; and the bishops in their mitres and rich robes, each with his pastoral staff in his hand, were standing round the altar. As the little Duke entered, there arose from all the voices in the chancel the full loud clear chant of *Te Deum Laudamus,* echoing among the dark vaults of the roof. To that sound Richard walked up the choir to a large, heavy, cross-legged, carved chair, raised on two steps, just before the steps of the altar began, and there he stood, Bernard de Harcourt and Eric de Centeville on each side of him, and all his other vassals in due order in the choir.

After the beautiful chant of the hymn was

ended, the service for the Holy Communion
began. When the time came for the offering,
each noble gave gold or silver; and, lastly,
Rainulf of Ferrières came up to the step of
the altar with a cushion, on which was placed
a circlet of gold, the ducal coronet; and another baron, following him closely, carried a
long heavy sword with a cross handle. The
Archbishop of Rouen received both coronet
and sword, and laid them on the altar. Then
the service proceeded. At that time the rite
of Confirmation was administered in infancy,
and Richard, who had been confirmed by his
godfather, the Archbishop of Rouen, immediately after his baptism, knelt in solemn awe
to receive the other Holy Sacrament from his
hands, as soon as all the clergy had commu-
nicated.

When the administration was over, Richard
was led forward to the step of the altar
by Count Bernard and Sir Eric, and the
Archbishop, laying one hand upon both his as
he held them clasped together, demanded of
him, in the name of God and of the people of

Normandy, whether he would be their good and true ruler, guard them from their foes, maintain truth, punish iniquity, and protect the Church.

"I will!" answered Richard's young trembling voice, "so help me God!" and he knelt and kissed the book of the Holy Gospels, which the Archbishop offered him.

It was a great and awful oath, and he dreaded to think that he had taken it. He still knelt, put both hands over his face, and whispered, "O God, my Father, help me to keep it."

The Archbishop waited till he rose, and then, turning him with his face to the people, said, "Richard, by the grace of God, I invest thee with the ducal mantle of Normandy!"

Two of the bishops then hung round his shoulders a crimson velvet mantle, furred with ermine, which, made as it was for a grown man, hung heavily on the poor child's shoulders, and lay in heaps on the ground. The Archbishop then set the golden coronet on his long, flowing hair, where it hung so loosely on the little head that Sir Eric was obliged to put his hand to it to hold it safe; and lastly, the long, straight, two-handed sword was brought and placed in his hand, with another solemn bidding to use it ever in maintaining the right. It should have been girded to his side, but the great sword was so much taller than the little Duke that, as it stood upright by him, he was obliged to raise his arm to put it round the handle.

He then had to return to his throne, which was not done without some difficulty, encumbered as he was; but Osmond held up the train of his mantle, Sir Eric kept the coronet on his head, and he himself held fast and lovingly the sword, though the Count of Harcourt offered to carry it for him. He was lifted up to his throne, and then came the paying him homage; Alan, Duke of Brittany, was the first to kneel before him, and with his hand between those of the Duke, he swore to be his man, to obey him, and pay him feudal service for his dukedom of Brittany. In return, Richard swore to be his good lord, and to protect him from all his foes. Then followed Bernard the Dane, and many another, each repeating the same formulary, as their large rugged hands were clasped within those little soft fingers. Many a kind and loving eye was bent in compassion on the orphan child; many a strong voice faltered with earnestness as it pronounced the vow, and many a brave stalwart heart heaved with grief for the murdered father, and tears flowed down the war-worn cheeks which had met the fiercest storms of the northern ocean, as they bent before the young fatherless boy, whom they loved for the sake of his conquering grandfather, and his brave and pious father. Few Normans were there whose hearts did not glow at the touch of those small hands, with a love almost of a parent for their young Duke.

The ceremony of receiving homage lasted long, and Richard, though interested and touched at first, grew very weary; the crown and mantle were so heavy, the faces succeeded each other like figures in an endless dream, and the constant repetition of the same words was very tedious. He grew sleepy, he longed to jump up, to lean to the right or left, or to speak something besides that regular form. He gave one great yawn, but it brought him such a frown from the stern face of Bernard as quite to wake him for a few minutes, and make him sit upright, and receive the next vassal with as much attention as he had shown the first; but he looked imploringly at Sir Eric, as if to ask if it ever would be over. At last, far down among the barons, came one at whose sight Richard revived a little. It was a boy only a few years older than himself, perhaps about ten, with a pleasant brown face, black hair, and quick black eyes which glanced, with a look between friendliness and respect, up into the little Duke's gazing face. Richard listened eagerly for his name, and was refreshed at the sound of the boyish voice which pronounced, "I, Alberic de Montémar, am thy liegeman and vassal for my castle and barony of Montémar sur Epte."

When Alberic moved away, Richard followed him with his eye as far as he could to his place in the Cathedral, and was taken by surprise when he found the next baron kneeling before him.

The ceremony of homage came to an end at last, and Richard would fain have run all the way to the palace to shake off his weariness, but he was obliged to head the procession again; and even when he reached the castle hall his toils were not over, for there was a great state banquet spread out, and he had to sit in the high chair where he remembered climbing on his father's knee last Christmas-day, all the time that the barons feasted round and held grave converse. Richard's best comfort all this time was in watching Osmond de Centeville and Alberic de Montémar, who, with the other youths who were not yet knighted, were waiting on those who sat at the table. At last he grew so very weary that he fell fast asleep in the corner of his chair, and did not wake till he was startled by the rough voice of Bernard

de Harcourt, calling him to rouse up, and bid
the Duke of Brittany farewell.

"Poor child!" said Duke Alan, as Richard
rose up, startled, "he is over-wearied with this
day's work. Take care of him, Count Bernard; thou art a kindly nurse, but a rough
one for such a babe. Ha! my young lord,
your colour mantles at being called a babe;
I crave your pardon, for you are a fine spirit.
And hark you, Lord Richard of Normandy, I
have little cause to love your race, and little
right, I trow, had King Charles the Simple
to call us free Bretons liegemen to a race of
plundering Northern pirates. To Duke Rollo's
might, my father never gave his homage;
nay, nor did I yield it for all Duke William's
long sword, but I did pay it to his generosity
and forbearance, and now I grant it to thy
weakness, and to his noble memory. I doubt
not that the recreant Frank, Louis, whom he
restored to his throne, will strive to profit by
thy youth and helplessness, and should that
be, remember that thou hast no surer friend

than Alan of Brittany. Fare thee well, my young Duke."

"Farewell, sir," said Richard, willingly giving his hand to be shaken by his kind vassal, and watching him as Sir Eric attended him from the hall.

"Fair words, but I trust not the Breton," muttered Bernard; "hatred is deeply ingrained in them."

"He should know what the Frank king is made of," said Rainulf de Ferrières; "he was bred up with him in the days that they were both exiles at the court of King Ethelstane of England."

"Ay, and thanks to Duke William that either Louis or Alan are not exiles still. Now we shall see whose gratitude is worth most, the Frank's or the Breton's; I suspect the Norman valour will be the best to trust to."

"Yes, and how will Norman valour prosper without treasure? Who knows what gold is in the Duke's coffers?"

There was some consultation here in a low

voice, and the next thing Richard heard distinctly was that one of the nobles held up a silver chain and key, saying that they had been found on the Duke's neck, and that he had kept them, thinking that they doubtless led to something of importance.

"Oh yes!" said Richard eagerly, "I know it. He told me it was the key to his greatest treasure."

The Normans heard this with great interest, and it was resolved that several of the most trusted persons, among whom were the Archbishop of Rouen, Abbot Martin of Jumièges, and the Count of Harcourt, should go immediately in search of this precious hoard. Richard accompanied them up the narrow rough stone stairs to the large dark apartment where his father had slept. Though a prince's chamber, it had little furniture; a low uncurtained bed, a cross on a ledge near its head, a rude table, a few chairs, and two large chests, were all it contained. Harcourt tried the lid of one of the chests; it opened, and proved to be full of wearing apparel; he went to the other, which was smaller, much more carved, and ornamented with very handsome iron-work. It was locked, and putting in the key, it fitted, the lock turned, and the chest was opened. The Normans pressed eagerly to see their Duke's greatest treasure.

It was a robe of serge and a pair of sandals, such as were worn in the Abbey of Jumièges.

"Ha! is this all! What didst say, child?" cried Bernard the Dane, hastily.

"He told me it was his greatest treasure!" repeated Richard.

"And it was!" said Abbot Martin.

Then the good Abbot told them the history, part of which was already known to some of them. About five or six years before, Duke William had been hunting in the Forest of Jumièges, when he had suddenly come on the ruins of the Abbey, which had been wasted thirty or forty years previously by the sea-king Hasting. Two old monks, of the original brotherhood, still survived, and came forth to greet the Duke and offer him their hospitality.

5

"Ay!" said Bernard, "well do I remember their bread; we asked if it was made of fir-bark, like that of our brethren of Norway."

William, then an eager thoughtless young man, turned with disgust from this wretched fare, and throwing the old men some gold, galloped on to enjoy his hunting. In the course of the sport he was left alone, and encountered a wild boar, which threw him down, trampled on him, and left him stretched sense-less on the ground, severely injured. His companions coming up, carried him, as the nearest place of shelter, to the ruins of Jumièges, where the two old monks gladly received him in the remaining portion of their house. As soon as he recovered his senses he earnestly asked their pardon for his pride, and the scorn he had shown to the poverty and patient suffering which he should have reverenced.

William had always been a man who chose the good and refused the evil, but this accident, and the long illness that followed it, made him far more thoughtful and serious

It was a robe of serge and a pair of sandals.

than he had ever been before; he made preparing for death and eternity his first object, and thought less of his worldly affairs, his wars, and his ducal state. He rebuilt the old Abbey, endowed it richly, and sent for Martin himself from France to become the Abbot; he delighted in nothing so much as praying there, conversing with the Abbot, and hearing him read holy books; and he felt his temporal affairs, and the state and splendour of his rank, so great a temptation, that he had one day come to the Abbot and entreated to be allowed to lay them aside, and become a brother of the order. But Martin had refused to receive his vows. He had told him that he had no right to neglect or forsake the duties of the station to which God had appointed him; that it would be a sin to leave the post which had been given him to defend; and that the way marked out for him to serve God was by doing justice among his people, and using his power to defend the right. Not till he had done his allotted work, and his son was old enough to take his place as ruler of the Normans, might he cease from his active duties, quit the turmoil of the world, and seek the repose of the cloister. It was in this hope of peaceful retirement that William had delighted to treasure up the humble garments that he hoped one day to wear in peace and holiness.

"And oh! my noble Duke!" exclaimed Abbot Martin, bursting into tears as he finished his narration, "the Lord hath been very gracious unto thee. He has taken thee home to thy rest, long before thou didst dare to hope for it."

Slowly, and with subdued feelings, the Norman barons left the chamber. Richard, whom they seemed to have almost forgotten, wandered to the stairs, to find his way to the room where he had slept last night. He had not made many steps before he heard Osmond's voice say, "Here, my lord;" he looked up, saw a white cap at a doorway a little above him; he bounded up, and flew into Dame Astrida's outstretched arms.

How glad he was to sit in her lap, and lay

his wearied head on her bosom, while, with a worn-out voice, he exclaimed, "O Fru Astrida! I am very, very tired of being Duke of Normandy!"

CHAPTER IV

Richard of Normandy was very anxious to know more of the little boy whom he had seen among his vassals.

"Ah! the young Baron de Montémar," said Sir Eric. "I knew his father well, and a brave man he was, though not of Northern blood. He was warden of the marches of the Epte, and was killed by your father's side in the inroad of the Viscount de Cotentin,[1] at the time when you were born, Lord Richard."

"But where does he live? Shall I not see him again?"

"Montémar is on the bank of the Epte, in the domain that the French wrongfully claim from us. He lives there with his mother, and if he be not yet returned, you shall see him presently. Osmond, go you and seek out the

[1] An attack in which Riouf, Vicomte de Cotentin, placed Normandy in the utmost danger. He was defeated on the banks of the Seine, in a field still called the Pré de Bataille, on the very day of Richard's birth, so that the *Te Deum* was sung at once for the victory and the birth of the heir of Normandy.

lodging of the young Montémar, and tell him
the Duke would see him."

Richard had never had a playfellow of his
own age, and his eagerness to see Alberic de
Montémar was great. He watched from the
window, and at length beheld Osmond enter-
ing the court with a boy of ten years old by
his side, and an old grey-headed squire, with
a golden chain to mark him as a seneschal or
steward of the castle, walking behind.

Richard ran to the door to meet them, holding out his hand eagerly. Alberic uncovered
his bright dark hair, bowed low and grace-
fully, but stood as if he did not exactly know
what to do next. Richard grew shy at the
same moment, and the two boys stood looking at each other somewhat awkwardly. It
was easy to see that they were of different
races, so unlike were the blue eyes, flaxen
hair, and fair face of the young Duke to the
black flashing eyes and olive cheek of the
French vassal, who, though two years older,
was scarcely above him in height; and his
slight figure, well-proportioned, active and

agile as it was, did not give the same promise of strength as the round limbs and large-boned frame of Richard, which even now seemed likely to rival the gigantic stature of his grandfather, Earl Rollo, the Ganger.

For some minutes the little Duke and the young Baron surveyed each other without a word, and old Sir Eric did not improve matters by saying, "Well, Lord Duke, here he is. Have you no better greeting for him?"

"The children are shamefaced," said Fru Astrida, seeing how they both coloured. "Is your lady mother in good health, my young sir?"

Alberic blushed more deeply, bowed to the old northern lady, and answered fast and low in French, "I cannot speak the Norman tongue."

Richard, glad to say something, interpreted Fru Astrida's speech, and Alberic readily made courteous reply that his mother was well, and he thanked the Dame de Centeville, a French title which sounded new to Fru Astrida's ears. Then came the embarrass-

ment again, and Fru Astrida at last said,
"Take him out, Lord Richard, take him to
see the horses in the stables, or the hounds,
or what not."

Richard was not sorry to obey, so out they
went into the court of Rollo's Tower, and in
the open air the shyness went off. Richard
showed his own pony, and Alberic asked if
he could leap into the saddle without putting
his foot in the stirrup. No, Richard could
not; indeed, even Osmond had never seen it
done, for the feats of French chivalry had
scarcely yet spread into Normandy.

"Can you?" said Richard; "will you show
us?"

"I know I can with my own pony," said
Alberic, "for Bertrand will not let me mount
in any other way; but I will try with yours,
if you desire it, my lord."

So the pony was led out. Alberic laid one
hand on its mane, and vaulted on its back in a
moment. Both Osmond and Richard broke
out loudly into admiration. "Oh, this is nothing!" said Alberic. "Bertrand says it is

nothing. Before he grew old and stiff he could spring into the saddle in this manner fully armed. I ought to do this much better."

Richard begged to be shown how to perform the exploit, and Alberic repeated it; then Richard wanted to try, but the pony's patience would not endure any longer, and Alberic said he had learnt on a block of wood, and practised on the great wolf-hound. They wandered about a little longer in the court, and then climbed up the spiral stone stairs to the battlements at the top of the tower, where they looked at the house-tops of Rouen close beneath, and the river Seine, broadening and glittering on one side in its course to the sea, and on the other narrowing to a blue ribbon winding through the green expanse of fertile Normandy. They threw the pebbles and bits of mortar down that they might hear them fall, and tried which could stand nearest to the edge of the battlement without being giddy. Richard was pleased to find that he could go the nearest, and began to tell some of Fru Astrida's stories about the precipices of Norway, among which when she was a young girl she used to climb about and tend the cattle in the long light summer time. When the two boys came down again into the hall to dinner they felt as if they had known each other all their lives. The dinner was laid out in full state, and Richard had, as before, to sit in the great throne-like chair, with the old Count of Harcourt on one side; but, to his comfort, Fru Astrida was on the other.

After the dinner, Alberic de Montémar rose to take his leave, as he was to ride half way to his home that afternoon. Count Bernard, who all dinner time had been watching him intently from under his shaggy eyebrows, at this moment turned to Richard, whom he hardly ever addressed, and said to him, "Hark ye, my lord, what should you say to have him yonder for a comrade?"

"To stay with me?" cried Richard, eagerly. "Oh, thanks, Sir Count; and may he stay?"

"You are lord here."

"O Alberic!" cried Richard, jumping out of his chair of state, and running up to him, "will you not stay with me, and be my brother and comrade?"

Alberic looked down, hesitating.

"Oh, say that you will! I will give you horses, and hawks, and hounds, and I will love you—almost as well as Osmond. Oh, stay with me, Alberic."

"I must obey you, my lord," said Alberic, "but——"

"Come, young Frenchman, out with it," said Bernard, "no buts! Speak honestly, and at once, like a Norman, if you can."

This rough speech seemed to restore the little Baron's self-possession, and he looked up bright and bold at the rugged face of the old Dane, while he said, "I had rather not stay here."

"Ha! not to do service to your lord?"

"I would serve him with all my heart, but I do not want to stay here. I love the Castle of Montémar better, and my mother has no one but me."

"Brave and true, Sir Frenchman," said the old Count, laying his great hand on

Alberic's head, and looking better pleased than Richard thought his grim features could have appeared. Then turning to Bertrand, Alberic's seneschal, he said, "Bear the Count de Harcourt's greetings to the noble Dame de Montémar, and say to her that her son is of a free bold spirit, and if she would have him bred up with my Lord Duke, as his comrade and brother in arms, he will find a ready welcome."

"So, Alberic, you will come back perhaps," said Richard.

"That must be as my mother pleases," answered Alberic bluntly, and with all due civilities he and his seneschal departed.

Four or five times a day did Richard ask Osmond and Fru Astrida if they thought Alberic would return, and it was a great satisfaction to him to find that every one agreed that it would be very foolish in the Dame de Montémar to refuse so good an offer, only Fru Astrida could not quite believe she would part with her son. Still no Baron de Montémar arrived, and the little Duke was beginning to think less about his hopes when one evening, as he was returning from a ride with Sir Eric and Osmond, he saw four horsemen coming towards them, and a little boy in front.

"It is Alberic himself, I am sure of it!" he exclaimed, and so it proved; and while the seneschal delivered his lady's message to Sir Eric, Richard rode up and greeted the welcome guest.

"Oh, I am very glad your mother has sent you!"

"She said she was not fit to bring up a young warrior of the Marches," said Alberic. "Were you very sorry to come?"

"I dare say I shall not mind it soon, and Bertrand is to come and fetch me home to visit her every three months, if you will let me go, my lord."

Richard was extremely delighted, and thought he could never do enough to make Rouen pleasant to Alberic, who after the first day or two cheered up, missed his mother less, managed to talk something between French

and Norman to Sir Eric and Fru Astrida,
and became a very animated companion and
friend. In one respect Alberic was a better
playfellow for the Duke than Osmond de
Centeville, for Osmond, playing as a grown-
up man, not for his own amusement, but the
child's, had left all the advantages of the
game to Richard, who was growing not a
little inclined to domineer. This Alberic did
not like, unless, as he said, "it was to be always lord and vassal, and then he did not
care for the game," and he played with so
little animation that Richard grew vexed.

"I can't help it," said Alberic; "if you take
all the best chances to yourself, 'tis no sport
for me. I will do your bidding, as you are the
Duke, but I cannot like it."

"Never mind my being Duke, but play as
we used to do."

"Then let us play as I did with Bertrand's
sons at Montémar. I was their Baron, as
you are my Duke, but my mother said there
would be no sport unless we forgot all that at
play."

"Then so we will. Come, begin again, Alberic, and you shall have the first turn."

However, Alberic was quite as courteous and respectful to the Duke when they were not at play as the difference of their rank required; indeed he had learnt much more of grace and courtliness of demeanour from his mother, a Provencal lady, than was yet to be found among the Normans. The chaplain of Montémar had begun to teach him to read and write, and he liked learning much better than Richard, who would not have gone on with Father Lucas's lessons at all, if Abbot Martin of Jumièges had not put him in mind that it had been his father's especial desire.

What Richard most disliked was, however, the being obliged to sit in council. The Count of Harcourt did in truth govern the dukedom, but nothing could be done without the Duke's consent, and, once a week at least, there was held in the great hall of Rollo's Tower what was called a *Parlement,* or a "talkation," where Count Bernard, the Archbishop, the Baron de Centeville, the Abbot of Jumièges,

6

and such other bishops, nobles, or abbots as might chance to be at Rouen, consulted on the affairs of Normandy; and there the little Duke always was forced to be present, sitting up in his chair of state, and hearing, rather than listening to, questions about the repairing and guarding of castles, the asking of loans from the vassals, the appeals from the Barons of the Exchequer, who were then nobles sent through the duchy to administer justice, and the discussions about the proceedings of his neighbours, King Louis of France, Count Foulques of Anjou, and Count Herluin of Montreuil, and how far the friendship of Hugh of Paris and Alan of Brittany might be trusted.

Very tired of all this did Richard grow, especially when he found that the Normans had made up their minds not to attempt a war against the wicked Count of Flanders. He sighed most wearily, yawned again and again, and moved restlessly about in his chair; but whenever Count Bernard saw him doing so, he received so severe a look and

sign that he grew perfectly to dread the eye
of the fierce old Dane. Bernard never spoke
to him to praise him, or to enter into any of
his pursuits; he only treated him with the
grave distant respect due to him as a prince,
or else now and then spoke a few stern words
to him, of reproof for this restlessness, or for
some other childish folly.

Used as Richard was to be petted and made
much of by the whole house of Centeville, he
resented this considerably in secret, disliked
and feared the old Count, and more than once
told Alberic de Montémar that as soon as he
was fourteen, when he would be declared of
age, he should send Count Bernard to take
care of his own castle of Harcourt, instead of
letting him sit gloomy and grim in the castle
hall in the evening, spoiling all their sport.

Winter had set in, and Osmond used daily
to take the little Duke and Alberic to the
nearest sheet of ice, for the Normans still
prided themselves on excelling in skating,
though they had long since left the frost-
bound streams and lakes of Norway.

One day, as they were returning from the ice, they were surprised, even before they entered the castle court, by hearing the trampling of horses' feet and a sound of voices.

"What may this mean?" said Osmond. "There must surely be a great arrival of the vassals. The Duke of Brittany, perhaps."

"Oh," said Richard, piteously, "we have had one council already this week. I hope another is not coming!"

"It must import something extraordinary," proceeded Osmond. "It is a mischance that the Count of Harcourt is not at Rouen just now."

Richard thought this no mischance at all, and just then, Alberic, who had run on a little before, came back exclaiming, "They are French. It is the Frank tongue, not the Norman, that they speak."

"So please you, my lord," said Osmond, stopping short, "we go not rashly into the midst of them. I would I knew what were best to do."

Osmond rubbed his forehead and stood

considering, while the two boys looked at him anxiously. In a few seconds, before he had come to any conclusion, there came forth from the gate a Norman squire, accompanied by two strangers.

"My Lord Duke," said he to Richard, in French, "Sir Eric has sent me to bring you tidings that the King of France has arrived to receive your homage."

"The King!" exclaimed Osmond.

"Ay!" proceeded the Norman, in his own tongue, "Louis himself, and with a train looking bent on mischief. I wish it may portend good to my lord here. You see I am accompanied. I believe from my heart that Louis meant to prevent you from receiving a warning, and taking the boy out of his clutches."

"Ha! what?" said Richard, anxiously. "Why is the King come? What must I do?"

"Go on now, since there is no help for it," said Osmond. "Greet the King as becomes you, bend the knee, and pay him homage."

Richard repeated over to himself the form

of homage that he might be perfect in it, and walked on into the court, Alberic, Osmond, and the rest falling back as he entered. The court was crowded with horses and men, and it was only by calling out loudly, "The Duke, the Duke!" that Osmond could get space enough for them to pass. In a few moments Richard had mounted the steps and stood in the great hall.

In the chair of state, at the upper end of the room, sat a small spare man, of about eight- or nine-and-twenty, pale, and of a light complexion, with a rich dress of blue and gold. Sir Eric and several other persons stood respectfully round him, and he was conversing with the Archbishop, who, as well as Sir Eric, cast several anxious glances at the little Duke as he advanced up the hall. He came up to the King, put his knee to the ground, and was just beginning, "Louis, King of France, I——" when he found himself suddenly lifted from the ground in the King's arms, and kissed on both cheeks. Then setting him on his knee, the King exclaimed,

"And is this the son of my brave and noble friend, Duke William? Ah! I should have known it from his likeness! Let me embrace you again, dear child, for your father's sake!"

Richard was rather overwhelmed, but he thought the King very kind, especially when Louis began to admire his height and free-spirited bearing, and to lament that his own sons, Lothaire and Carloman, were so much smaller and more backward. He caressed Richard again and again, praised every word he said—Fru Astrida was nothing to him; and Richard began to say to himself how strange and unkind it was of Bernard de Harcourt to like to find fault with him, when on the contrary he deserved all this praise from the King himself.

CHAPTER V

Duke Richard of Normandy slept in the room which had been his father's; Alberic de Montémar, as his page, slept at his feet, and Osmond de Centeville had a bed on the floor, across the door, where he lay with his sword close at hand, as his young lord's guard and protector.

All had been asleep for some little time, when Osmond was startled by a slight movement of the door, which could not be pushed open without awakening him. In an instant he had grasped his sword, while he pressed his shoulder to the door to keep it close; but it was his father's voice that answered him with a few whispered words in the Norse tongue, "It is I; open." He made way instantly, and old Sir Eric entered, treading cautiously with bare feet, and sat down on the bed, motioning him to do the same, so that they might be able to speak lower. "Right, Osmond," he said. "It is well to be on the alert, for peril enough is around him—the Frank means mischief! I know from a sure hand that Arnulf of Flanders was in council with him just before he came hither, with his false tongue, wiling and coaxing the poor child!"

"Ungrateful traitor!" murmured Osmond. "Do you guess his purpose?"

"Yes, surely; to carry the boy off with him, and so he trusts doubtless to cut off all the race of Rollo! I know his purpose is to bear off the Duke, as a ward of the crown, forsooth. Did you not hear him luring the child with his promises of friendship with the Princes? I could not understand all his French words, but I saw it plain enough."

"You will never allow it?"

"If he does, it must be across our dead bodies; but taken as we are by surprise, our resistance will little avail. The castle is full of French, the hall and court swarm with them. Even if we could draw our Normans together, we should not be more than a dozen men, and what could we do but die? That we are ready for, if it may not be otherwise, rather than let our charge be thus borne off without a pledge for his safety, and without the knowledge of the states."

"The King could not have come at a worse time," said Osmond.

"No, just when Bernard the Dane is absent. If he only knew what has befallen, he could raise the country, and come to the rescue."

"Could we not send some one to bear the tidings to-night?"

"I know not," said Sir Eric musingly. "The French have taken the keeping of the doors; indeed, they are so thick through the castle that I can hardly reach one of our men, nor could I spare one hand that may avail to guard the boy to-morrow."

"Sir Eric——" a little bare foot was heard on the floor, and Alberic de Montémar stood before him. "I did not mean to listen, but I could not help hearing you. I cannot fight for the Duke yet, but I could carry a message."

"How would that be?" said Osmond eagerly. "Once out of the castle, and in Rouen, he could easily find means of sending to the Count. He might go either to the Convent of St. Ouen, or, which would be better, to the trusty armourer Thibault, who would soon find man and horse to send after the Count."

"Ha! Let me see," said Sir Eric. "It might be. But how is he to get out?"

"I know a way," said Alberic. "I scrambled down that wide buttress by the east wall last week, when our ball was caught in a branch of the ivy, and the drawbridge is down."

"If Bernard knew, it would be off my mind, at least!" said Sir Eric. "Well, my young Frenchman, you may do good service."

"Osmond," whispered Alberic, as he began hastily to dress himself, "only ask one thing of Sir Eric—never to call me 'young Frenchman' again!"

Sir Eric smiled, saying, "Prove yourself Norman, my boy."

"Then," added Osmond, "if it were possible to get the Duke himself out of the Castle tomorrow morning, if I could take him forth by the postern, and once bring him into the town, he would be safe. It would be only to raise the burghers, or else to take refuge in the Church of Our Lady till the Count came up, and then Louis would find his prey out of nis hands when he awoke and sought him."

"That might be," replied Sir Eric; "but I doubt your success. The French are too eager to hold him fast, to let him slip out of their hands. You will find every door guarded."

"Yes, but all the French have not seen the Duke, and the sight of a squire and a little page going forth will scarcely excite their suspicion."

"Ay, if the Duke would bear himself like a little page, but that you need not hope for. Besides, he is so taken with this King's flatteries that I doubt whether he would consent to leave him for the sake of Count Bernard. Poor child, he is like to be soon taught to know his true friends."

"I am ready," said Alberic, coming forward.

The Baron de Centeville repeated his in-

Osmond went with him softly down the stairs.

structions, and then undertook to guard the
door, while his son saw Alberic set off on his
expedition. Osmond went with him softly
down the stairs, then avoiding the hall, which
was filled with French, they crept silently to
a narrow window, guarded by iron bars,
placed at such short intervals apart that only
so small and slim a form as Alberic's could
have squeezed out between them. The distance to the ground was not much more than
twice his own height, and the wall was so covered with ivy that it was not a very dangerous feat for an active boy, so that Alberic was
soon safe on the ground; then looking up to
wave his cap, he ran on along the side of the
moat, and was soon lost to Osmond's sight in
the darkness.

Osmond returned to the Duke's chamber,
and relieved his father's guard, while Richard
slept soundly on, little guessing at the plots
of his enemies, or at the schemes of his faithful subjects for his protection.

Osmond thought this all the better, for he
had small trust in Richard's patience and

self-command, and thought there was much more chance of getting him unnoticed out of the castle, if he did not know how much depended on it, and how dangerous his situation was.

When Richard awoke, he was much surprised at missing Alberic, but Osmond said he was gone into the town to Thibault the armourer, and this was a message on which he was so likely to be employed, that Richard's suspicion was not excited. All the time he was dressing he talked about the King, and everything he meant to show him that day; then, when he was ready, the first thing was as usual to go to attend morning mass.

"Not by that way to-day, my lord," said Osmond, as Richard was about to enter the great hall. "It is crowded with the French who have been sleeping there all night; come to the postern."

Osmond turned, as he spoke, along the passage, walking fast, and not sorry that Richard was lingering a little, as it was safer for him to be first. The postern was, as he expected, guarded by two tall steel-cased figures, who immediately held their lances across the doorway, saying, "None passes without warrant."

"You will surely let us of the castle attend to our daily business," said Osmond. "You will hardly break your fast this morning if you stop all communication with the town."

"You must bring warrant," repeated one of the men-at-arms. Osmond was beginning to say that he was the son of the seneschal of the castle, when Richard came hastily up. "What? Do these men want to stop us?" he exclaimed in the imperious manner he had begun to take up since his accession. "Let us go on, sirs."

The men-at-arms looked at each other, and guarded the door more closely. Osmond saw it was hopeless, and only wanted to draw his young charge back without being recognised, but Richard exclaimed loudly, "What means this?"

"The King has given orders that none

should pass without warrant," was Osmond's answer. "We must wait."

"I will pass!" said Richard, impatient at opposition to which he was little accustomed. "What mean you, Osmond? This is my castle, and no one has a right to stop me. Do you hear, grooms? Let me go. I am the Duke!"

The sentinels bowed, but all they said was, "Our orders are express."

"I tell you I am Duke of Normandy, and I will go where I please in my own city!" exclaimed Richard, passionately pressing against the crossed staves of the weapons, to force his way between them, but he was caught and held fast in the powerful gauntlet of one of the men-at-arms. "Let me go, villain!" cried he, struggling with all his might. "Osmond, Osmond, help!"

Even as he spoke, Osmond had disengaged him from the grasp of the Frenchman, and putting his hand on his arm, said, "Nay, my lord, it is not for you to strive with such as these."

"I will strive!" cried the boy. "I will not

have my way barred in my own castle. I will
tell the King how these rogues of his use me.
I will have them in the dungeon. Sir Eric!
where is Sir Eric?"

Away he rushed to the stairs, Osmond
hurrying after him lest he should throw himself into some fresh danger, or by his loud
calls attract the French, who might then
easily make him prisoner. However, on the
very first step of the stairs stood Sir Eric,
who was too anxious for the success of the
attempt to escape, to be very far off. Richard,
too angry to heed where he was going, dashed
up against him without seeing him, and as
the old Baron took hold of him, began, "Sir
Eric, Sir Eric, those French are villains! they
will not let me pass—"

"Hush, hush, my lord," said Sir Eric.
"Silence! come here."

However imperious with others, Richard
from force of habit always obeyed Sir Eric,
and now allowed himself to be dragged hastily and silently by him, Osmond following
closely, up the stairs, up a second and a third

winding flight, still narrower, and with
broken steps, to a small round thick-walled
turret chamber, with an extremely small
door, and loopholes of windows, high up in
the tower. Here, to his great surprise, he
found Dame Astrida, kneeling and telling her
beads, two or three of her maidens, and about
four of the Norman squires and men-at-
arms.

"So you have failed, Osmond?" said the
Baron.

"But what is all this? How did Fru
Astrida come up here? May I not go to the
King and have all those insolent Franks
punished?"

"Listen to me, Lord Richard," said Sir
Eric; "that smooth-spoken King whose words
so charmed you last night is an ungrateful
deceiver. The Franks have always hated and
feared the Normans, and not being able to
conquer us fairly, they now take to foul
means. Louis came hither from Flanders; he
has brought this great troop of French to surprise us, claim you as a ward of the crown,

and carry you away with him to some prison
of his own."

"You will not let me go?" said Richard.

"Not while I live," said Sir Eric. "Alberic
is gone to warn the Count of Harcourt, to call
the Normans together, and here we are ready
to defend this chamber to our last breath;
but we are few, the French are many, and
succour may be far off."

"Then you meant to have taken me out of
their reach this morning, Osmond?"

"Yes, my lord."

"And if I had not flown into a passion and
told who I was, I might have been safe! O
Sir Eric! Sir Eric! you will not let me be carried off to a French prison!"

"Here, my child," said Dame Astrida, holding out her arms; "Sir Eric will do all he can
for you, but we are in God's hands!"

Richard came and leant against her. "I
wish I had not been in a passion!" said he
sadly, after a silence; then looking at her in
wonder—"But how came you up all this
way?"

"It is a long way for my old limbs," said Fru Astrida, smiling, "but my son helped me, and he deems it the only safe place in the castle."

"The safest," said Sir Eric, "and that is not saying much for it."

"Hark!" said Osmond, "what a tramping the Franks are making. They are beginning to wonder where the Duke is."

"To the stairs, Osmond," said Sir Eric. "On that narrow step one man may keep them at bay a long time. You can speak their jargon too, and hold parley with them."

"Perhaps they will think I am gone," whispered Richard, "if they cannot find me, and go away."

Osmond and two of the Normans were, as he spoke, taking their stand on the narrow spiral stair, where there was just room for one man on the step. Osmond was the lowest, the other two above him, and it would have been very hard for an enemy to force his way past them.

Osmond could plainly hear the sounds of

the steps and voices of the French as they consulted together, and sought for the Duke. A man at length was heard clanking up these very stairs, till winding round, he suddenly found himself close upon young de Centeville.

"Ha! Norman!" he cried, starting back in amazement, "what are you doing here?"

"My duty," answered Osmond, shortly. "I am here to guard this stair;" and his drawn sword expressed the same intention.

The Frenchman drew back, and presently a whispering below was heard, and soon after a voice came up the stairs, saying, "Norman— good Norman——"

"What would you say?" replied Osmond, and the head of another Frank appeared. "What means all this, my friend?" was the address. "Our King comes as a guest to you, and you received him last night as loyal vassals. Wherefore have you now drawn out of the way, and striven to bear off your young Duke into secret places? Truly it looks not well that you should thus strive to keep him apart, and therefore the King requires to see him instantly."

"Sir Frenchman," replied Osmond, "your King claims the Duke as his ward. How that may be my father knows not, but as he was committed to his charge by the states of Normandy, he holds himself bound to keep him in his own hands until further orders from them."

"That means, insolent Norman, that you intend to shut the boy up and keep him in your own rebel hands. You had best yield—it will be the better for you and for him. The child is the King's ward, and he shall not be left to be nurtured in rebellion by northern pirates."

At this moment a cry from without arose, so loud as almost to drown the voices of the speakers on the turret stair, a cry welcome to the ears of Osmond, repeated by a multitude of voices, "Haro! Haro! our little Duke!"

It was well known as a Norman shout. So just and so ready to redress all grievances had the old Duke Rollo been, that his very name was an appeal against injustice, and whenever wrong was done, the Norman outcry against the injury was always "Ha Rollo!" or, as it had become shortened, "Haro." And now Osmond knew that those whose affection had been won by the uprightness of Rollo were gathering to protect his helpless grandchild.

The cry was likewise heard by the little garrison in the turret chamber, bringing hope and joy. Richard thought himself already rescued, and springing from Fru Astrida, danced about in ecstasy, only longing to see the faithful Normans, whose voices he heard ringing out again and again, in calls for their little Duke, and outcries against the Franks. The windows were, however, so high, that nothing could be seen from them but the sky; and, like Richard, the old Baron de Centeville was almost beside himself with anxiety to know what force was gathered together, and what measures were being taken. He opened the door, called to his son, and asked if he could tell what was passing; but Osmond knew as little, he could see nothing but the black, cobwebbed, dusty steps winding above his head, while the clamours outside, waxing fiercer and louder, drowned all the sounds which might otherwise have come up to him from the French within the castle. At last, however, Osmond called out to his father, in Norse, "There is a Frank Baron come to entreat, and this time very humbly, that the Duke may come to the King."

"Tell him," replied Sir Eric, "that save with consent of the council of Normandy, the child leaves not my hands."

"He says," called back Osmond, after a moment, "that you shall guard him yourself, with as many as you choose to bring with you. He declares on the faith of a free Baron, that the King has no thought of ill—he wants to show him to the Rouennais without, who are calling for him, and threaten to tear down the tower rather than not see their little Duke. Shall I bid him send a hostage?"

"Answer him," returned the Baron, "that the Duke leaves not this chamber unless a pledge is put into our hands for his safety.

There was an oily-tongued Count, who sat next the King at supper—let him come hither, and then perchance I may trust the Duke among them."

Osmond gave the desired reply, which was carried to the King. Meantime the uproar outside grew louder than ever, and there were new sounds, a horn was winded, and there was a shout of *"Dieu Aide,"* the Norman war-cry, joined with "Notre Dame de Harcourt!"

"There, there!" cried Sir Eric, with a long breath, as if relieved of half his anxieties, "the boy has sped well. Bernard is here at last! now his head and hand are there, I doubt no longer."

"Here comes the Count," said Osmond, opening the door, and admitting a stout burly man, who seemed sorely out of breath with the ascent of the steep broken stairs, and very little pleased to find himself in such a situation. The Baron de Centeville augured well from the speed with which he had been sent, thinking it proved great perplexity and distress on the part of Louis. Without waiting to hear his hostage speak, he pointed to a chest on which he had been sitting, and bade two of his men-at-arms stand on each side of the Count, saying at the same time to Fru Astrida, "Now, mother, if aught of evil befalls the child, you know your part. Come, Lord Richard."

Richard moved forward. Sir Eric held his hand. Osmond kept close behind him, and with as many of the men-at-arms as could be spared from guarding Fru Astrida and her hostage, he descended the stairs, not by any means sorry to go, for he was weary of being besieged in that turret chamber, whence he could see nothing, and with those friendly cries in his ears, he could not be afraid.

He was conducted to the large council-room, which was above the hall. There, the King was walking up and down anxiously, looking paler than his wont, and no wonder, for the uproar sounded tremendous there—and now and then a stone dashed against the sides of the deep window.

Nearly at the same moment as Richard

entered by one door, Count Bernard de Harcourt came in from the other, and there was a slight lull in the tumult.

"What means this, my lords?" exclaimed the King. "Here am I come in all good will, in memory of my warm friendship with Duke William, to take on me the care of his orphan, and hold council with you for avenging his death, and is this the greeting you afford me? You steal away the child, and stir up the rascaille of Rouen against me. Is this the reception for your King?"

"Sir King," replied Bernard, "what your intentions may be, I know not. All I do know is, that the burghers of Rouen are fiercely incensed against you—so much so, that they were almost ready to tear me to pieces for being absent at this juncture. They say that you are keeping the child prisoner in his own castle, and that they will have him restored, if they tear it down to the foundations."

"You are a true man, a loyal man—you understand my good intentions," said Louis, trembling, for the Normans were extremely dreaded. "You would not bring the shame of rebellion on your town and people. Advise me —I will do just as you counsel me—how shall I appease them?"

"Take the child, lead him to the window, swear that you mean him no evil, that you will not take him from us," said Bernard. "Swear it on the faith of a King."

"As a King—as a Christian, it is true!" said Louis. "Here, my boy! Wherefore shrink from me? What have I done that you should fear me? You have been listening to evil tales of me, my child. Come hither."

At a sign from the Count de Harcourt, Sir Eric led Richard forward, and put his hand into the King's. Louis took him to the window, lifted him upon the sill, and stood there with his arm round him, upon which the shout, "Long live Richard, our little Duke!" arose again. Meantime the two Centevilles looked in wonder at the old Harcourt, who shook his head, and muttered in his own tongue, "I will do all I may, but our force is small, and the

King has the best of it. We must not yet bring a war on ourselves."

"Hark! he is going to speak," said Osmond.

"Fair Sirs—excellent burgesses!" began the King, as the cries lulled a little. "I rejoice to see the love ye bear to your young Prince—I would all my subjects were equally loyal! But wherefore dread me as if I were come to injure him? I, who came but to take counsel how to avenge the death of his father, who brought me back from England when I was a friendless exile. Know ye not how deep is the debt of gratitude I owe to Duke William? He it was who made me King—it was he who gained me the love of the King of Germany; he stood godfather for my son; to him I owe all my wealth and state; and all my care is to render guerdon for it to his child, since, alas! I may not to himself. Duke William rests in his bloody grave, it is for me to call his murderers to account, and to cherish his son even as mine own!"

So saying, Louis tenderly embraced the little boy, and the Rouennais below broke out into another cry in which "Long live King Louis!" was joined with "Long live Richard!"

"You will not let the child go?" said Eric meanwhile to Harcourt.

"Not without provision for his safety, but we are not fit for war as yet, and to let him go is the only means of warding it off."

Eric groaned and shook his head; but the Count de Harcourt's judgment was of such weight with him that he never dreamt of disputing it.

"Bring me here," said the King, "all that you deem most holy, and you shall see me pledge myself to be your Duke's most faithful friend."

There was some delay, during which the Norman nobles had time for further counsel together, and Richard looked wistfully at them, wondering what was to happen to him, and wishing he could venture to ask for Alberic.

Several of the clergy of the Cathedral presently appeared in procession, bringing with them the book of the Gospels on which Richard

had taken his installation oath, with others of
the sacred treasures of the church, preserved
in gold cases. The priests were followed by a
few of the Norman knights and nobles, some
of the burgesses of Rouen, and, to Richard's
great joy, by Alberic de Montémar himself.
The two boys stood looking eagerly at each
other, while preparation was made for the
ceremony of the King's oath.

The stone table in the middle of the room
was cleared and arranged so as in some degree to resemble the altar in the cathedral;
then the Count de Harcourt, standing before
it, and holding the King's hand, demanded of
him whether he would undertake to be the
friend, protector, and good lord of Richard,
Duke of Normandy, guarding him from all his
enemies, and ever seeking his welfare. Louis,
with his hand on the Gospels, swore that so
he would.

"Amen!" returned Bernard the Dane,
solemnly, "and as thou keepest that oath to
the fatherless child, so may the Lord do unto
thine house!"

Then followed the ceremony which had been interrupted the night before, of the homage and oath of allegiance which Richard owed to the King, and on the other hand the King's formal reception of him as a vassal holding under him the two dukedoms of Normandy and Brittany. "And," said the King, raising him in his arms and kissing him, "no dearer vassal do I hold in all my realm than this fair child, son of my murdered friend and benefactor—precious to me as my own children, as soon my Queen and I hope to testify."

Richard did not much like all this embracing; but he was sure the King really meant him no ill, and he wondered at all the distrust the Centevilles had shown.

"Now, brave Normans," said the King, "be ye ready speedily for an onset on the traitor Fleming. The cause of my ward is my own cause. Soon shall the trumpet be sounded, the ban and arrière ban of the realm be called forth, and Arnulf, in the flames of his cities, and the blood of his vassals, shall learn to rue the day when his foot trod the isle of Pec-

8

quigny! How many Normans can you bring to the muster, Sir Count?"

"I cannot say, within a few hundreds of lances," replied the old Dane cautiously; "it depends on the numbers that may be engaged in the Italian war with the Saracens; but of this be sure, Sir King, that every man in Normandy and Brittany who can draw a sword, or bend a bow, will stand forth in the cause of our little Duke; ay, and that his blessed father's memory is held so dear in our northern home that it needs but a message to King Harald Blue-tooth to bring a fleet of long keels into the Seine, with stout Danes enough to carry fire and sword, not merely through Flanders, but through all France. We of the north are not apt to forget old friendships and favours, Sir King."

"Yes, yes, I know the Norman faith of old," returned Louis uneasily, "but we should scarcely need such wild allies as you propose; the Count of Paris, and Hubert of Senlis may be reckoned on, I suppose."

"No truer friend to Normandy than gallant

and wise old Hugh the White!" said Bernard, "and as to Senlis, he is uncle to the boy, and doubly bound to us."

"I rejoice to see your confidence," said Louis. "You shall soon hear from me. In the meantime I must return to gather my force together, and summon my great vassals, and I will, with your leave, brave Normans, take with me my dear young ward. His presence will plead better in his cause than the finest words; moreover, he will grow up in love and friendship with my two boys, and shall be nurtured with them in all good learning and chivalry, nor shall he ever be reminded that he is an orphan while under the care of Queen Gerberge and myself."

"Let the child come to me, so please you, my lord the King," answered Harcourt bluntly. "I must hold some converse with him ere I can reply."

"Go then, Richard," said Louis, "go to your trusty vassal—happy are you in possessing such a friend; I hope you know his value."

"Here then, young sir," said the Count, in

his native tongue, when Richard had crossed
from the King's side, and stood beside him,
"what say you to this proposal?"

"The King is very kind," said Richard. "I
am sure he is kind; but I do not like to go from
Rouen, or from Dame Astrida."

"Listen, my lord," said the Dane, stooping
down and speaking low. "The King is resolved
to have you away; he has with him the best of
his Franks, and has so taken us at unawares,
that though I might yet rescue you from his
hands, it would not be without a fierce struggle,
wherein you might be harmed, and this castle
and town certainly burnt, and wrested from
us. A few weeks or months, and we shall have
time to draw our force together, so that Normandy need fear no man, and for that time
you must tarry with him."

"Must I—and all alone?"

"No, not alone, not without the most trusty
guardian that can be found for you. Friend
Eric, what say you?" and he laid his hand on
the old Baron's shoulder. "Yet I know not;
true thou art, as a Norwegian mountain, but

I doubt me if thy brains are not too dull to see through the French wiles and disguises, sharp as thou didst show thyself last night."

"That was Osmond, not I," said Sir Eric. "He knows their mincing tongue better than I. He were the best to go with the poor child, if go he must."

"Bethink you, Eric," said the Count, in an undertone. "Osmond is the only hope of your good old house—if there is foul play, the guardian will be the first to suffer."

"Since you think fit to peril the only hope of all Normandy, I am not the man to hold back my son where he may aid him," said old Eric sadly. "The poor child will be lonely and uncared-for there, and it were hard he should not have one faithful comrade and friend with him."

"It is well," said Bernard; "young as he is, I had rather trust Osmond with the child than any one else, for he is ready of counsel and quick of hand."

"Ay, and a pretty pass it is come to," muttered old Centeville, "that we, whose business it is to guard the boy, should send him where you scarcely like to trust my son."

Bernard paid no further attention to him, but, coming forward, required another oath from the King, that Richard should be as safe and free at his court as at Rouen, and that on no pretence whatsoever should he be taken from under the immediate care of his esquire, Osmond Fitz Eric, heir of Centeville.

After this, the King was impatient to depart, and all was preparation. Bernard called Osmond aside to give full instructions on his conduct, and the means of communicating with Normandy, and Richard was taking leave of Fru Astrida, who had now descended from her turret, bringing her hostage with her. She wept much over her little Duke, praying that he might safely be restored to Normandy, even though she might not live to see it; she exhorted him not to forget the good and holy learning in which he had been brought up, to rule his temper, and, above all, to say his prayers constantly, never leaving out one, as the beads of his rosary reminded him of their order. As to her own grandson, anxiety for him seemed almost lost in her fears for Richard, and the chief things she said to him, when he came to take leave of her, were directions as to the care he was to take of the child, telling him the honour he now received was one which would make his name for ever esteemed if he did but fulfil his trust, the most precious that Norman had ever yet received.

"I will, grandmother, to the very best of my power," said Osmond; "I may die in his cause, but never will I be faithless!"

"Alberic!" said Richard, "are you glad to be going back to Montémar?"

"Yes, my lord," answered Alberic sturdily, "as glad as you will be to come back to Rouen."

"Then I shall send for you directly, Alberic, for I shall never love the Princes Carloman and Lothaire half as well as you!"

"My lord the King is waiting for the Duke," said a Frenchman, coming forward.

"Farewell then, Fru Astrida. Do not weep. I shall soon come back. Farewell, Alberic. Take the bar-tailed falcon back to Montémar, and keep him for my sake. Farewell, Sir Eric —farewell, Count Bernard. When the Normans come to conquer Arnulf, you will lead them. O dear, dear Fru Astrida, farewell again."

"Farewell, my own darling. The blessing of Heaven go with you, and bring you safe home! Farewell, Osmond. Heaven guard you, and strengthen you to be his shield and defence!"

CHAPTER VI

Away from the tall narrow gateway of Rollo's
Tower, with the cluster of friendly sorrowful
faces looking forth from it, away from the
booth-like shops of Rouen, and the stout
burghers shouting with all the power of their
lungs, "Long live Duke Richard! Long live
King Louis! Death to the Fleming!"—away
from the broad Seine—away from home and
friends rode the young Duke of Normandy, by
the side of the palfrey of the King of France.

The King took much notice of him, kept him
by his side, talked to him, admired the beautiful cattle grazing in security in the green pastures, and as he looked at the rich dark brown
earth of the fields, the castles towering above
the woods, the convents looking like great
farms, the many villages round the rude
churches, and the numerous population who
came out to gaze at the party, and repeat the
cry of "Long live the King! Blessings on the

little Duke !" he told Richard, again and again, that his was the most goodly duchy in France, and Germany to boot.

When they crossed the Epte, the King would have Richard in the same boat with him, and sitting close to Louis, and talking eagerly about falcons and hounds, the little Duke passed the boundary of his own dukedom.

The country beyond was not like Normandy. First they came to a great forest, which seemed to have no path through it. The King ordered that one of the men, who had rowed them across, should be made to serve as guide, and two of the men-at-arms took him between them, and forced him to lead the way, while others with their swords and battle-axes cut down and cleared away the tangled branches and briars that nearly choked the path. All the time every one was sharply on the look-out for robbers, and the weapons were all held ready for use at a moment's notice. On getting beyond the forest, a castle rose before them, and though it was not yet late in the day, they resolved to rest there, as a marsh lay not far before them, which it would not have been safe to traverse in the evening twilight.

The Baron of the castle received them with great respect to the King, but without paying much attention to the Duke of Normandy, and Richard did not find the second place left for him at the board. He coloured violently, and looked first at the King, and then at Osmond, but Osmond held up his finger in warning; he remembered how he had lost his temper before, and what had come of it, and resolved to try to bear it better; and just then the Baron's daughter, a gentle-looking maiden of fifteen or sixteen, came and spoke to him, and entertained him so well that he did not think much more of his offended dignity.

When they set off on their journey again, the Baron and several of his followers came with them to show the only safe way across the morass, and a very slippery, treacherous, quaking road it was, where the horses' feet left pools of water wherever they trod. The King and the Baron rode together, and the

other French nobles closed round them;
Richard was left quite in the background, and
though the French men-at-arms took care not
to lose sight of him, no one offered him any
assistance, excepting Osmond, who, giving his
own horse to Sibald, one of the two Norman
grooms who accompanied him, led Richard's
horse by the bridle along the whole distance
of the marshy path, a business that could
scarcely have been pleasant, as Osmond wore
his heavy hauberk, and his pointed iron-
guarded boots sank deep at every step into
the bog. He spoke little, but seemed to be taking good heed of every stump of willow, or
stepping-stone, that might serve as note of
remembrance of the path.

At the other end of the morass began a long
tract of dreary-looking heathy waste, without
a sign of life. The Baron took leave of the
King, only sending three men-at-arms to show
him the way to a monastery, which was to be
the next halting-place. He sent three, because
it was not safe for one, even fully armed, to
ride alone, for fear of the attacks of the fol-

Osmond led Richard's horse by the bridle.

lowers of a certain marauding Baron, who was at deadly feud with him, and made all that border a most perilous region. Richard might well observe that he did not like the Vexin half as well as Normandy, and that the people ought to learn Fru Astrida's story of the golden bracelets, which in his grandfather's time had hung untouched for a year in a tree in a forest.

It was pretty much the same through the whole journey, waste lands, marshes, and forests alternated. The castles stood on high mounds frowning on the country round, and villages were clustered round them, where the people either fled away, driving off their cattle with them, at the first sight of an armed band, or else, if they remained, proved to be thin, wretched-looking creatures, with wasted limbs, aguish faces, and often iron collars round their necks. Wherever there was anything of more prosperous appearance, such as a few cornfields, vineyards on the slopes of the hills, fat cattle, and peasantry looking healthy and secure, there was sure to be seen

a range of long low stone buildings, surmounted with crosses, with a short square
church tower rising in the midst, and interspersed with gnarled hoary old apple-trees, or
with gardens of pot-herbs spreading before
them to the meadows. If, instead of two or
three men-at-arms from a castle, or of some
trembling serf pressed into the service, and
beaten, threatened, and watched to prevent
treachery, the King asked for a guide at a
convent, some lay brother would take his staff,
or else mount an ass, and proceed in perfect
confidence and security as to his return home-
wards, sure that his poverty and his sacred
character would alike protect him from any
outrage from the most lawless marauder of
the neighbourhood.

Thus they travelled until they reached the
royal castle of Laon, where the Fleur-de-Lys
standard on the battlements announced the
presence of Gerberge, Queen of France, and
her two sons. The King rode first into the
court with his nobles, and before Richard
could follow him through the narrow arched

gateway, he had dismounted, entered the castle, and was out of sight. Osmond held the Duke's stirrup, and followed him up the steps which led to the castle hall. It was full of people, but no one made way, and Richard, holding his squire's hand, looked up in his face, inquiring and bewildered.

"Sir Seneschal," said Osmond, seeing a broad portly old man, with grey hair and a golden chain, "this is the Duke of Normandy —I pray you conduct him to the King's presence."

Richard had no longer any cause to complain of neglect, for the seneschal instantly made him a very low bow, and calling "Place —place for the high and mighty prince, my Lord Duke of Normandy!" ushered him up to the dais or raised part of the floor, where the King and Queen stood together talking. The Queen looked round as Richard was announced, and he saw her face, which was sallow and with a sharp sour expression that did not please him; and he backed and looked reluctant, while Osmond, with a warning hand pressed on his shoulder, was trying to remind him that he ought to go forward, kneel on one knee, and kiss her hand.

"There he is," said the King.

"One thing secure!" said the Queen; "but what makes that northern giant keep close to his heels?"

Louis answered something in a low voice, and, in the meantime, Osmond tried in a whisper to induce his young lord to go forward and perform his obeisance.

"I tell you I will not," said Richard. "She looks cross, and I do not like her."

Luckily he spoke his own language; but his look and air expressed a good deal of what he said, and Gerberge looked all the more unattractive.

"A thorough little Norwegian bear," said the King; "fierce and unruly as the rest. Come and perform your courtesy—do you forget where you are?" he added sternly.

Richard bowed, partly because Osmond forced down his shoulder; but he thought of old Rollo, and Charles the Simple, and his

9

proud heart resolved that he would never kiss
the hand of that sour-looking Queen. It was
a determination made in pride and defiance,
and he suffered for it afterwards; but no more
passed now, for the Queen only saw in his be-
haviour that of an unmannerly young Northman; and though she disliked and despised
him, she did not care enough about his courtesy to insist on its being paid. She sat down,
and so did the King, and they went on talking;
the King probably telling her his adventures
at Rouen, while Richard stood on the step of
the dais, swelling with sullen pride.

Nearly a quarter of an hour had passed in
this manner, when the servants came to set
the tables for supper, and Richard, in spite of
his indignant looks, was forced to stand aside.
He wondered that all this time he had not seen
the two Princes, thinking how strange he
should have thought it, to let his own dear
father be in the house so long without coming
to welcome him. At last, just as the supper
had been served up, a side door opened, and
the seneschal called, "Place for the high and

mighty Princes, my Lord Lothaire, and my
Lord Carloman!" and in walked two boys, one
about the same age as Richard, the other
rather less than a year younger. They were
both thin, pale, sharp-featured children, and
Richard drew himself up to his full height
with great satisfaction at being so much taller
than Lothaire.

They came up ceremoniously to their father
and kissed his hand, while he kissed their fore-
heads, and then said to them, "There is a new
playfellow for you."

"Is that the little Northman?" said Carloman, turning to stare at Richard with a look
of curiosity, while Richard in his turn felt
considerably affronted that a boy so much less
than himself should call him little.

"Yes," said the Queen, "your father has
brought him home with him."

Carloman stepped forward, shyly holding
out his hand to the stranger, but his brother
pushed him rudely aside, "I am the eldest; it
is my business to be first. So, young Northman, you are come here for us to play with?"

Richard was too much amazed at being
spoken to in this imperious way to make any
answer. He was completely taken by surprise,
and only opened his great blue eyes to their
utmost extent.

"Ha! why don't you answer? Don't you
hear? Can you speak only your own heathen
tongue?" continued Lothaire.

"The Norman is no heathen tongue!" said
Richard, at once breaking silence in a loud
voice. "We are as good Christians as you are,
ay, and better too."

"Hush! hush! my lord!" said Osmond.

"What now, Sir Duke," again interfered the
King, in an angry tone, "are you brawling already? Time, indeed, I should take you from
your own savage court. Sir squire, look to it
that you keep your charge in better rule,
or I shall send him instantly to bed supper-
less."

"My lord, my lord," whispered Osmond, "see
you not that you are bringing discredit on all
of us?"

"I would be courteous enough, if they would

be courteous to me," returned Richard, gazing with eyes full of defiance at Lothaire, who, returning an angry look, had nevertheless shrunk back to his mother. She meanwhile was saying, "So strong, so rough the young savage is, he will surely harm our poor boys!"

"Never fear," said Louis; "he shall be watched. And," he added, in a lower tone, "for the present at least, we must keep up appearances. Hubert of Senlis and Hugh of Paris have their eyes on us, and were the boy to be missed, the grim old Harcourt would have all the pirates of his land on us in the twinkling of an eye. We have him, and there we must rest content for the present. Now to supper."

At supper Richard sat next little Carloman, who peeped at him every now and then from under his eyelashes, as if he was afraid of him; and presently, when there was a good deal of talking going on, so that his voice could not be heard, half whispered in a very grave tone, "Do you like salt beef or fresh?"

"I like fresh," answered Richard, with equal gravity, "only we eat salt all the winter."

There was another silence, and then Carloman, with the same solemnity, asked, "How old are you?"

"I shall be nine on the eve of St. Boniface. How old are you?"

"Eight. I was eight at Martinmas, and Lothaire was nine three days since."

Another silence; then as Osmond waited on Richard, Carloman returned to the charge: "Is that your squire?"

"Yes, that is Osmond de Centeville."

"How tall he is!"

"We Normans are taller than you French."

"Don't say so to Lothaire, or you will make him angry."

"Why? It is true."

"Yes, but," and Carloman sank his voice, "there are some things which Lothaire will not hear said. Do not make him cross, or he will make my mother displeased with you. She caused Thierry de Lincourt to be scourged, because his ball hit Lothaire's face."

"She cannot scourge me, I am a free Duke," said Richard. "But why? Did he do it on purpose?"

"Oh, no!"

"And was Lothaire hurt?"

"Hush! you must say Prince Lothaire. No, it was quite a soft ball."

"Why?" again asked Richard, "why was he scourged?"

"I told you, because he hit Lothaire."

"Well, but did he not laugh, and say it was nothing? Alberic quite knocked me down with a great snowball the other day, and Sir Eric laughed, and said I must stand firmer."

"Do you make snowballs?"

"To be sure I do. Do not you?"

"Oh, no! the snow is so cold."

"Ah! you are but a little boy," said Richard in a superior manner. Carloman asked how it was done, and Richard gave an animated description of the snow-balling a fortnight ago at Rouen, when Osmond and some of the other young men built a snow fortress, and defended it against Richard, Alberic, and the other squires. Carloman listened with delight, and declared that next time it snowed, they would have a snow castle; and thus by the time supper was over, the two little boys were very good friends.

Bedtime came not long after supper. Richard's was a smaller room than he had been used to at Rouen; but it amazed him exceedingly when he first went into it; he stood gazing in wonder, because, as he said, "it was as if he had been in a church."

"Yes, truly!" said Osmond. "No wonder these poor creatures of French cannot stand before a Norman lance, if they cannot sleep without glass to their windows. Well! what would my father say to this?"

"And see! see, Osmond! they have put hangings up all round the walls, just like Our Lady's church on a great feast-day. They treat us just as if we were the holy saints; and here are fresh rushes strewn about the floor too. This must be a mistake, it must be an oratory instead of my chamber."

"No, no, my lord; here is our gear, which I

bade Sibald and Henry see bestowed in our chamber. Well, these Franks are come to a pass indeed! my grandmother will never believe what we shall have to tell her. Glass windows and hangings to sleeping chambers! I do not like it—I am sure we shall never be able to sleep, closed up from the free air of heaven in this way; I shall be always waking and fancying I am in the chapel at home, hearing Father Lucas chanting his matins. Besides, my father would blame me for letting you be made as tender as a Frank. I'll have out this precious window if I can."

Luxurious as the young Norman thought the King, the glazing of Laon was not permanent. It consisted of casements, which could be put up or removed at pleasure, for as the court possessed only one set of glass windows, they were taken down and carried from place to place, as often as Louis removed from Rheims to Soissons, Laon, or any of his other royal castles; so that Osmond did not find much difficulty in displacing them, and letting in the sharp cold wintry breeze. The next thing he did was to give his young lord a lecture on his want of courtesy, telling him "that no wonder the Franks thought he had no more culture than a Viking (or pirate), fresh caught from Norway. A fine notion he was giving them of the training he had at Centeville, if he could not even show common civility to the Queen, a lady! Was that the way Alberic had behaved when he came to Rouen?"

"Fru Astrida did not make sour faces at him, nor call him a young savage," replied Richard.

"No, and he gave her no reason to do so; he knew that the first teaching of a young knight is to be courteous to ladies, never mind whether fair and young, or old and foul of favour. Till you learn and note that, Lord Richard, you will never be worthy of your golden spurs."

"And the King told me she would treat me as a mother," exclaimed Richard. "Do you think the King speaks the truth, Osmond?"

"That we shall see by his deeds," said Osmond.

"He was very kind while we were in Normandy. I loved him so much better than the Count de Harcourt; but now I think the Count is best! I'll tell you, Osmond, I will never call him grim old Bernard again."

"You had best not, sir, for you never will have a more true-hearted vassal."

"Well! I wish we were back in Normandy, with Fru Astrida and Alberic. I cannot bear that Lothaire. He is proud, and unknightly, and cruel, I am sure he is, and I will never love him."

"Hush, my lord! Beware of speaking so loud. You are not in your own castle."

"And Carloman is a chicken-heart," continued Richard, unheeding. "He does not like to touch snow, and he cannot even slide on the ice, and he is afraid to go near that great dog —that beautiful wolf-hound."

"He is very little," said Osmond.

"I am sure I was not as cowardly at his age, now was I, Osmond? Don't you remember?"

"Come, Lord Richard, I cannot let you wait to remember everything; tell your beads, and

pray that we may be brought safe back to
Rouen; and that you may not forget all the
good that Father Lucas and holy Abbot
Martin have laboured to teach you."

So Richard told the beads of his rosary—
black polished wood, with amber at certain
spaces; he repeated a prayer with every bead,
and Osmond did the same; then the little Duke
put himself into a narrow crib of richly carved
walnut; while Osmond having stuck his dagger so as to form an additional bolt to secure
the door, and examined the hangings that no
secret entrance might be concealed behind
them, gathered a heap of rushes together, and
lay down on them, wrapped in his mantle,
across the doorway. The Duke was soon
asleep; but the squire lay long awake, musing
on the possible dangers that surrounded his
charge, and on the best way of guarding
against them.

CHAPTER VII

Osmond de Centeville was soon convinced that
no immediate peril threatened his young Duke
at the court of Laon. Louis seemed to intend
to fulfil his oaths to the Normans by allowing
the child to be the companion of his own sons,
and to be treated in every respect as became
his rank. Richard had his proper place at
table, and all due attendance; he learnt, rode,
and played with the Princes, and there was
nothing to complain of excepting the coldness
and inattention with which the King and
Queen treated him, by no means fulfilling the
promise of being as parents to their orphan
ward. Gerberge, who had from the first
dreaded his superior strength and his roughness with her puny boys, and who had been
by no means won by his manners at their first
meeting, was especially distant and severe
with him, hardly ever speaking to him except
with some rebuke, which, it must be confessed,
Richard often deserved.

As to the boys, his constant companions, Richard was on very friendly terms with Carloman, a gentle, timid, weakly child. Richard looked down upon him, but he was kind, as a generous-tempered boy could not fail to be, to one younger and weaker than himself. He was so much kinder than Lothaire, that Carloman was fast growing very fond of him, and looked up to his strength and courage as something noble and marvellous.

It was very different with Lothaire, the person from whom, above all others, Richard would have most expected to meet with affection, as his father's godson, a relationship which, in those times, was thought almost as near as kindred by blood. Lothaire had been brought up by an indulgent mother, and by courtiers who never ceased flattering him as the heir to the crown, and he had learnt to think that to give way to his naturally imperious and violent disposition was the way to prove his power and assert his rank. He had always had his own way, and nothing had ever been done to check his faults; somewhat

weakly health had made him fretful and timid;
and a latent consciousness of this fearfulness
made him all the more cruel, sometimes because he was frightened, sometimes because
he fancied it manly.

He treated his little brother in a way which
in these times boys would call bullying; and,
as no one ever dared to oppose the King's
eldest son, it was pretty much the same with
every one else, except now and then some
dumb creature, and then all Lothaire's cruelty
was shown. When his horse kicked, and
ended by throwing him, he stood by, and
caused it to be beaten till the poor creature's
back streamed with blood; when his dog bit
his hand in trying to seize the meat with
which he was teasing it, he insisted on having
it killed, and it was worse still when a falcon
pecked one of his fingers. It really hurt him a
good deal, and, in a furious rage, he caused
two nails to be heated red-hot in the fire, in-
tending to have them thrust into the poor
bird's eyes.

"I will not have it done!" exclaimed Richard,

expecting to be obeyed as he was at home; but Lothaire only laughed scornfully, saying, "Do you think you are master here, sir pirate?"

"I will not have it done!" repeated Richard. "Shame on you, shame on you, for thinking of such an unkingly deed."

"Shame on me! Do you know to whom you speak, master savage?" cried Lothaire, red with passion.

"I know who is the savage now!" said Richard. "Hold!" to the servant who was bringing the red-hot irons in a pair of tongs.

"Hold?" exclaimed Lothaire. "No one commands here but I and my father. Go on, Charlot—where is the bird? Keep her fast, Giles."

"Osmond! You I can command——"

"Come away, my lord," said Osmond, interrupting Richard's order before it was issued. "We have no right to interfere here, and cannot hinder it. Come away from such a foul sight."

"Shame on you too, Osmond, to let such a deed be done without hindering it!" exclaimed Richard, breaking from him, and rushing on the man who carried the hot irons. The French servants were not very willing to exert their strength against the Duke of Normandy, and Richard's onset, taking the man by surprise, made him drop the tongs. Lothaire, both afraid and enraged, caught them up as a weapon of defence, and, hardly knowing what he did, struck full at Richard's face with the hot iron. Happily it missed his eye, and the heat had a little abated; but as it touched his cheek it burnt him sufficiently to cause considerable pain. With a cry of passion, he flew at Lothaire, shook him with all his might, and ended by throwing him at his length on the pavement. But this was the last of Richard's exploits, for he was at the same moment captured by his squire, and borne off, struggling and kicking as if Osmond had been his greatest foe; but the young Norman's arms were like iron round him; and he gave over his resistance sooner, because at that moment a whirring, flapping sound was heard, and the poor hawk rose high, higher, over their heads in ever lessening circles, far away from her

10

enemies. The servant who held her had relaxed his grasp in the consternation caused by
Lothaire's fall, and she was mounting up and
up, spying, it might be, her way to her native
rocks in Iceland, with the yellow eyes which
Richard had saved.

"Safe! safe!" cried Richard joyfully, ceas-
ing his struggles. "Oh, how glad I am! That
young villain should never have hurt her. Put
me down, Osmond; what are you doing with
me?"

"Saving you from your—no, I cannot call it
folly; I would hardly have had you stand still
to see such— But let me see your face."

"It is nothing. I don't care now the hawk is
safe," said Richard, though he could hardly
keep his lips in order, and was obliged to wink
very hard with his eyes to keep the tears out,
now that he had leisure to feel the smarting.
But it would have been far beneath a Northman to complain, and he stood bearing it gal-
lantly, and pinching his fingers tightly together, while Osmond knelt down to examine
the hurt. " 'Tis not much," said he, talking to

himself, "half bruise, half burn—I wish my grandmother was here—however, it can't last long! 'Tis right, you bear it like a little Berserker, and it is no bad thing that you should have a scar to show, that they may not be able to say you did *all* the damage."

"Will it always leave a mark?" said Richard. "I am afraid they will call me Richard of the Scarred Cheek, when we get back to Normandy."

"Never mind if they do—it will not be a mark to be ashamed of, even if it does last, which I do not believe it will."

"Oh no, I am so glad the gallant falcon is out of his reach!" replied Richard, in a somewhat quivering voice.

"Does it smart much? Well, come and bathe it with cold water—or shall I take you to one of the Queen's women?"

"No—the water," said Richard, and to the fountain in the court they went; but Osmond had only just begun to splash the cheek with the half-frozen water, with a sort of rough kindness, afraid at once of teaching the Duke to be effeminate, and of not being as tender to him as Dame Astrida would have wished, when a messenger came in haste from the King, commanding the presence of the Duke of Normandy and his squire.

Lothaire was standing between his father and mother on their throne-like seat, leaning against the Queen, who had her arm round him; his face was red and glazed with tears, and he still shook with subsiding sobs. It was evident he was just recovering from a passionate crying fit.

"How is this?" began the King, as Richard entered. "What means this conduct, my Lord of Normandy? Know you what you have done in striking the heir of France? I might imprison you this instant in a dungeon, where you would never see the light of day."

"Then Bernard de Harcourt would come and set me free," fearlessly answered Richard.

"Do you bandy words with me, child? Ask Prince Lothaire's pardon instantly, or you shall rue it."

"I have done nothing to ask his pardon for. It would have been cruel and cowardly in me to let him put out the poor hawk's eyes," said Richard, with a Northman's stern contempt for pain, disdaining to mention his own burnt cheek, which indeed the King might have seen plainly enough.

"Hawk's eyes!" repeated the King. "Speak the truth, Sir Duke; do not add slander to your other faults."

"I have spoken the truth—I always speak it!" cried Richard. "Whoever says otherwise lies in his throat!"

Osmond here hastily interfered, and desired permission to tell the whole story. The hawk was a valuable bird, and Louis's face darkened when he heard what Lothaire had purposed, for the Prince had, in telling his own story, made it appear that Richard had been the aggressor by insisting on letting the falcon fly. Osmond finished by pointing to the mark on Richard's cheek, so evidently a burn as to be proof that hot iron had played a part in the matter. The King looked at one of his own

squires and asked his account, and he with
some hesitation could not but reply that it was
as the young Sieur de Centeville had said.
Thereupon Louis angrily reproved his own
people for having assisted the Prince in trying to injure the hawk, called for the chief
falconer, rated him for not better attending
to his birds, and went forth with him to
see if the hawk could yet be recaptured,
leaving the two boys neither punished nor
pardoned.

"So you have escaped for this once," said
Gerberge coldly to Richard; "you had better
beware another time. Come with me, my poor
darling Lothaire." She led her son away to
her own apartments, and the French squires
began to grumble to each other complaints of
the impossibility of pleasing their lords, since,
if they contradicted Prince Lothaire, he was
so spiteful that he was sure to set the Queen
against them, and that was far worse in the
end than the King's displeasure. Osmond, in
the meantime, took Richard to recommence
bathing his face, and presently Carloman ran

out to pity him, wonder at him for not crying, and say he was glad the poor hawk had escaped.

The cheek continued inflamed and painful for some time, and there was a deep scar long after the pain had ceased, but Richard thought little of it after the first, and would have scorned to bear ill-will to Lothaire for the injury.

Lothaire left off taunting Richard with his Norman accent, and calling him a young sea-king. He had felt his strength, and was afraid of him; but he did not like him the better—he never played with him willingly—scowled, and looked dark and jealous, if his father or any of the great nobles took the least notice of the little Duke, and whenever he was out of hearing, talked against him with all his natural spitefulness.

Richard liked Lothaire quite as little, contemning almost equally his cowardly ways and his imperious disposition. Since he had been Duke, Richard had been somewhat inclined to grow imperious himself, though always kept

under restraint by Fru Astrida's good training and Count Bernard's authority, and his
whole generous nature would have revolted
against treating Alberic, or indeed his mean-
est vassal, as Lothaire used the unfortunate
children who were his playfellows. Perhaps
this made him look on with great horror at the
tyranny which Lothaire exercised; at any rate
he learnt to abhor it more, and to make many
resolutions against ordering people about un-
civilly when once he should be in Normandy
again. He often interfered to protect the poor
boys, and generally with success, for the
Prince was afraid of provoking such another
shake as Richard had once given him, and
though he generally repaid himself on his vic-
tim in the end, he yielded for the time.

Carloman, whom Richard often saved from
his brother's unkindness, clung closer and
closer to him, went with him everywhere, tried
to do all he did, grew very fond of Osmond,
and liked nothing better than to sit by Richard
in some wide window-seat, in the evening after
supper, and listen to Richard's version of some

of Fru Astrida's favourite tales, or hear the
never-ending history of sports at Centeville,
or at Rollo's Tower, or settle what great
things they would both do when they were
grown-up, and Richard was ruling Normandy
—perhaps go to the Holy Land together, and
slaughter an unheard-of host of giants and
dragons on the way. In the meantime, however, poor Carloman gave small promise of
being able to perform great exploits, for he
was very small for his age and often ailing,
soon tired, and never able to bear much rough
play. Richard, who had never had any reason
to learn to forbear, did not at first understand
this, and made Carloman cry several times
with his roughness and violence, but this always vexed him so much that he grew careful
to avoid such things for the future, and grad-
ually learnt to treat his poor little weakly
friend with a gentleness and patience at
which Osmond used to marvel, and which he
would hardly have been taught in his pros-
perity at home.

Between Carloman and Osmond, he was

thus tolerably happy at Laon, but he missed
his own dear friends and the loving greetings
of his vassals, and longed earnestly to be at
Rouen, asking Osmond almost every night
when they should go back; to which Osmond
could only answer that he must pray that
Heaven would be pleased to bring them home
safely.

Osmond, in the meantime, kept a vigilant
watch for anything that might seem to
threaten danger to his lord; but at present
there was no token of any evil being intended;
the only point in which Louis did not seem to
be fulfilling his promises to the Normans was,
that no preparations were made for attacking
the Count of Flanders.

At Easter, the court was visited by Hugh
the White, the great Count of Paris, the most
powerful man in France, and who was only
prevented by his own loyalty and forbearance
from taking the crown from the feeble and
degenerate race of Charlemagne. He had
been a firm friend of William Longsword, and
Osmond remarked how, on his arrival, the

King took care to bring Richard forward,
talk of him affectionately, and caress him almost as much as he had done at Rouen. The
Count himself was really kind and affectionate
to the little Duke; he kept him by his side, and
seemed to like to stroke down his long flaxen
hair, looking in his face with a grave mournful expression, as if seeking for a likeness to
his father. He soon asked about the scar
which the burn had left, and the king was
obliged to answer hastily, it was an accident,
a disaster that had chanced in a boyish quar-
rel. Louis, in fact, was uneasy, and appeared
to be watching the Count of Paris the whole
time of his visit, so as to prevent him from
having any conversation in private with the
other great vassals assembled at the court.
Hugh did not seem to perceive this, and acted
as if he was entirely at his ease, but at the
same time he watched his opportunity. One
evening after supper he came up to the window where Richard and Carloman were, as
usual, deep in story-telling; he sat down on
the stone seat, and taking Richard on his knee,

he asked if he had any greetings for the Count de Harcourt.

How Richard's face lighted up! "Oh, sir," he cried, "are you going to Normandy?"

"Not yet, my boy, but it may be that I may have to meet old Harcourt at the Elm of Gisors."

"Oh, if I was but going with you!"

"I wish I could take you, but it would scarcely do for me to steal the heir of Normandy. What shall I tell him?"

"Tell him," whispered Richard, edging himself close to the Count, and trying to reach his ear, "tell him that I am sorry, now, that I was sullen when he reproved me. I know he was right. And, sir, if he brings with him a certain huntsman with a long hooked nose, whose name is Walter,[1] tell him I am sorry I used to order him about so unkindly. And tell him to bear my greetings to Fru Astrida and Sir Eric, and to Alberic."

[1] In a battle fought with Lothaire at Charmenil, Richard saved the life of Walter the huntsman, who had been with him from his youth.

"Oh, sir, are you going to Normandy?"

"Shall I tell him how you have marked your face?"

"No," said Richard, "he would think me a baby to care about such a thing as that!"

The Count asked how it happened, and Richard told the story, for he felt as if he could tell the kind Count anything, it was almost like that last evening that he had sat on his father's knee. Hugh ended by putting his arm round him, and saying, "Well, my little Duke, I am as glad as you are the gallant bird is safe—it will be a tale for my own little Hugh and Eumacette[1] at home—and you must one day be friends with them as your father has been with me. And now, do you think your squire could come to my chamber late this evening when the household is at rest?"

Richard undertook that Osmond should do so, and the Count, setting him down again, returned to the dais. Osmond, before going

[1] At fourteen years of age, Richard was betrothed to Eumacette of Paris, then but eight years old. In such esteem did Hugues le blanc hold his son-in-law, that on his death-bed he committed his son Hugues Capet to his guardianship, though the Duke was then scarcely above twenty, proposing him as the model of wisdom and of chivalry.

to the Count that evening, ordered Sibald to come and guard the Duke's door. It was a long conference, for Hugh had come to Laon chiefly for the purpose of seeing how it went with his friend's son, and was anxious to know what Osmond thought of the matter. They agreed that at present there did not seem to be any evil intended, and that it rather appeared as if Louis wished only to keep him as a hostage for the tranquillity of the borders of Normandy; but Hugh advised that Osmond should maintain a careful watch, and send intelligence to him on the first token of mischief.

The next morning the Count of Paris quitted Laon, and everything went on in the usual course till the feast of Whitsuntide, when there was always a great display of splendour at the French court. The crown vassals generally came to pay their duty and go with the King to church; and there was a state banquet, at which the King and Queen wore their crowns, and every one sat in great magnificence according to his rank.

The grand procession to church was over. Richard had walked with Carloman, the Prince richly dressed in blue, embroidered with golden fleur-de-lys, and Richard in scarlet, with a gold cross on his breast. The beautiful service was over, they had returned to the castle, and there the seneschal was marshalling the goodly and noble company to the banquet, when horses' feet were heard at the gate, announcing some fresh arrival. The seneschal went to receive the guests, and presently was heard ushering in the noble Prince, Arnulf, Count of Flanders!

Richard's face became pale—he turned from Carloman, by whose side he had been standing, and walked straight out of the hall and up the stairs, closely followed by Osmond. In a few minutes there was a knock at the door of his chamber, and a French knight stood there saying, "Comes not the Duke to the banquet?"

"No," answered Osmond; "he eats not with the slayer of his father."

"The King will take it amiss; for the sake

of the child, you had better beware," said the Frenchman, hesitating.

"He had better beware himself," exclaimed Osmond indignantly, "how he brings the treacherous murderer of William Longsword into the presence of a free-born Norman, unless he would see him slain where he stands. Were it not for the boy, I would challenge the traitor this instant to single combat."

"Well, I can scarce blame you," said the knight, "but you had best have a care how you tread. Farewell."

Richard had hardly time to express his indignation, and his wishes that he was a man, before another message came through a groom of Lothaire's train, that the Duke must fast, if he would not consent to feast with the rest.

"Tell Prince Lothaire," replied Richard, "that I am not such a glutton as he—I had rather fast than be choked with eating with Arnulf!"

All the rest of the day, Richard remained in his own chamber, resolved not to run the

11

risk of meeting with Arnulf. The squire remained with him in this voluntary imprisonment, and they occupied themselves as best they could, with furbishing Osmond's armour, and helping each other out in repeating some of the Sagas. They once heard a great uproar in the court, and both were very anxious to learn its cause, but they did not know it till late in the afternoon.

Carloman crept up to them—"Here I am at last!" he exclaimed. "Here, Richard, I have brought you some bread, as you had no dinner; it was all I could bring. I saved it under the table lest Lothaire should see it."

Richard thanked Carloman with all his heart, and, being very hungry, was glad to share the bread with Osmond. He asked how long the wicked Count was going to stay, and rejoiced to hear he was going away the next morning, and the King was going with him.

"What was that great noise in the court?" asked Richard.

"I scarcely like to tell you," returned Carloman.

Richard, however, begged to hear, and Carloman was obliged to tell that the two Norman grooms, Sibald and Henry, had quarrelled with the Flemings of Arnulf's train; there had been a fray, which had ended in the death of three Flemings, a Frank, and of Sibald himself. And where was Henry? Alas! there was more ill news: the King had sentenced Henry to die, and he had been hanged immediately.

Dark with anger and sorrow grew young Richard's face. He had been fond of his two Norman attendants, he trusted to their attachment, and he would have wept for their loss even if it had happened in any other way; but now, when it had been caused by their enmity to his father's foes, the Flemings, when one had fallen overwhelmed by numbers, and the other been condemned hastily, cruelly, unjustly, it was too much, and he almost choked with grief and indignation. Why had he not been there, to claim Henry as his own vassal, and if he could not save him, at least bid him farewell? Then he would have broken out in angry threats, but he felt his own helplessness, and was ashamed, and he could only shed tears of passionate grief, refusing all Carloman's attempts to comfort him. Osmond was even more concerned; he valued the two Normans extremely for their courage and faithfulness, and had relied on sending intelligence by their means to Rouen in case of need. It appeared to him as if the first opportunity had been seized of removing these protectors from the little Duke, and as if the designs, whatever they might be, which had been formed against him, were about to take effect. He had little doubt that his own turn would be the next; but he was resolved to endure anything rather than give the smallest opportunity of removing him, to bear even insults with patience, and to remember that in his care rested the sole hope of safety for his charge.

That danger was fast gathering round them became more evident every day, especially after the King and Arnulf had gone away together. It was very hot weather, and Richard began to weary after the broad cool river at Rouen, where he used to bathe last

summer; and one evening he persuaded his
squire to go down with him to the Oise, which
flowed along some meadow ground about a
quarter of a mile from the castle; but they
had hardly set forth before three or four attendants came running after them, with express orders from the Queen that they should
return immediately. They obeyed, and found
her standing in the castle hall, looking greatly
incensed.

"What means this?" she asked angrily.
"Knew you not that the King has left commands that the Duke quits not the castle in
his absence?"

"I was only going as far as the river——"
began Richard, but Gerberge cut him short.

"Silence, child, I will hear no excuses. Perhaps you think, Sieur de Centeville, that you
may take liberties in the King's absence, but
I tell you that if you are found without the
walls again it shall be at your peril; ay, and
his! I'll have those haughty eyes put out if
you disobey."

She turned away, and Lothaire looked at

them with his air of gratified malice. "You will not lord it over your betters much longer, young pirate," said he, as he followed his mother, afraid to stay to meet the anger he might have excited by the taunt he could not deny himself the pleasure of making; but Richard, who six months ago could not brook a slight disappointment or opposition, had, in his present life of restraint, danger, and vexation, learnt to curb the first outbreak of temper, and to bear patiently instead of breaking out into passion and threats, and now his only thought was of his beloved squire.

"O Osmond! Osmond!" he exclaimed, "they shall not hurt you. I will never go out again; I will never speak another hasty word; I will never affront the Prince if they will but leave you with me!"

CHAPTER VIII

It was a fine summer evening, and Richard and Carloman were playing at ball on the steps of the castle gate, when a voice was heard from beneath, begging for alms from the noble Princes in the name of the Blessed Virgin, and the two boys saw a pilgrim standing at the gate, wrapped in a long robe of serge, with a staff in his hand, surmounted by a cross, a scrip at his girdle, and a broad shady hat, which he had taken off, as he stood, making low obeisances and asking charity.

"Come in, holy pilgrim," said Carloman; "it is late, and you shall sup and rest here to-night."

"Blessings from Heaven light on you, noble Prince," replied the pilgrim, and at that moment Richard shouted joyfully, "A Norman, a Norman! 'tis my own dear speech! Oh, are you not from Normandy? Osmond, Osmond, he comes from home!"

"My lord! my own lord!" exclaimed the

pilgrim, and, kneeling on one knee at the foot of the steps, he kissed the hand which his young Duke held out to him—"This is joy unlooked-for!"

"Walter! Walter the huntsman!" cried Richard. "Is it you? Oh! how is Fru Astrida, and all at home?"

"Well, my lord, and wearying to know how it is with you——" began Walter; but a very different tone exclaimed from behind the pilgrim, "What is all this? Who is stopping my way? What! Richard would be King, and more, would he? More insolence!" It was Lothaire, returning with his attendants from the chase, in by no means an amiable mood, for he had been disappointed of his game.

"He is a Norman—a vassal of Richard's own," said Carloman.

"A Norman, is he? I thought we had got rid of the robbers! We want no robbers here! Scourge him soundly, Perron, and teach him how to stop my way!"

"He is a pilgrim, my lord," suggested one of the followers.

"I care not; I'll have no Normans here, coming spying in disguise. Scourge him, I say, dog that he is! Away with him! A spy, a spy!"

"No Norman is scourged in my sight!" said Richard, darting forwards, and throwing himself between Walter and the woodsman, who was preparing to obey Lothaire, just in time to receive on his own bare neck the sharp, cutting leathern thong, which raised a long red streak along its course. Lothaire laughed.

"My Lord Duke—What have you done? O leave me—this befits you not!" cried Walter, extremely distressed; but Richard had caught hold of the whip, and called out, "Away, away! run! haste, haste!" and the words were repeated at once by Osmond, Carloman, and many of the French, who, though afraid to disobey the Prince, were unwilling to violate the sanctity of a pilgrim's person. And the Norman, seeing there was no help for it, obeyed; the French made way for him, and he effected his escape, while Lothaire, after a great deal of storming and raging, went up to his mother to triumph in the cleverness with which he had detected a Norman spy in disguise.

Lothaire was not far wrong; Walter had really come to satisfy himself as to the safety of the little Duke, and try to gain an interview with Osmond. In the latter purpose he failed, though he lingered in the neighbourhood of Laon for several days; for Osmond never left the Duke for an instant, and he was, as has been shown, a close prisoner, in all but the name, within the walls of the castle. The pilgrim had, however, the opportunity of picking up tidings which made him perceive the true state of things; he learnt the deaths of Sibald and Henry, the alliance between the King and Arnulf, and the restraint and harshness with which the Duke was treated; and with this intelligence he went in haste to Normandy.

Soon after his arrival, a three days' fast was observed throughout the dukedom, and in every church, from the Cathedral of Bayeux to the smallest and rudest village shrine, crowds of worshippers were kneeling, imploring, many of them with tears, that God would look on them in His mercy, restore to them their Prince, and deliver the child out of the hands of his enemies. How earnest and sorrowful were the prayers offered at Centeville may well be imagined; and at Montémar sur Epte the anxiety was scarcely less. Indeed, from the time the evil tidings arrived, Alberic grew so restless and unhappy, and so anxious to do something, that at last his mother set out with him on a pilgrimage to the Abbey of Jumièges, to pray for the rescue of his dear little Duke.

In the meantime Louis had sent notice to Laon that he should return home in a week's time; and Richard rejoiced at the prospect, for the King had always been less unkind to him than the Queen, and he hoped to be released from his captivity within the castle. Just at this time he became very unwell; it might have been only the effect of the life of unwonted confinement which he had lately led that was beginning to tell on his health, but after being heavy and uncomfortable for a day or two without knowing what was the matter with him, he was one night attacked with high fever.

Osmond was dreadfully alarmed, knowing nothing at all of the treatment of illness, and, what was worse, fully persuaded that the poor child had been poisoned, and therefore re- solved not to call any assistance. He hung over him all night, expecting each moment to see him expire, ready to tear his hair with despair and fury, and yet obliged to restrain himself to the utmost quietness and gentleness to soothe the suffering of the sick child.

Through that night Richard either tossed about on his narrow bed, or, when his rest- lessness desired the change, sat, leaning his aching head on Osmond's breast, too op- pressed and miserable to speak or think.

When the day dawned on them, and he was still too ill to leave the room, messengers were sent for him, and Osmond could no longer conceal the fact of his sickness, but parleyed at the door, keeping out every one he could, and refusing all offers of attendance. He would not even admit Carloman, though Richard, hearing his voice, begged to see him; and when a proposal was sent from the Queen that a skilful old nurse should visit and prescribe for the patient, he refused with all his might, and when he had shut the door, walked up and down, muttering, "Ay, ay, the witch! coming to finish what she has begun!"

All that day and the next Richard continued very ill, and Osmond waited on him very assiduously, never closing his eyes for a moment, but constantly telling his beads whenever the boy did not require his attendance. At last Richard fell asleep, slept long and soundly for some hours, and waked much better. Osmond was in a transport of joy.

"Thanks to Heaven, they shall fail for this time! and they shall never have another chance. May Heaven be with us still!"

Richard was too weak and weary to ask what he meant, and for the next few days Osmond watched him with the utmost care. As for food, now that Richard could eat again, Osmond would not hear of his touching what was sent for him from the royal table, but always went down himself to procure food in the kitchen, where he said he had a friend among the cooks, who would, he thought, scarcely poison him intentionally. When Richard was able to cross the room, he insisted on his always fastening the door with his dagger, and never opening to any summons but his own, not even to Prince Carloman's. Richard wondered, but he was obliged to obey; and he knew enough of the perils around him to perceive the reasonableness of Osmond's caution.

Thus several days had passed, the King had returned, and Richard was so much recovered that he had become very anxious to be

allowed to go downstairs again, instead of
remaining shut up there; but still Osmond
would not consent, though Richard had done
nothing all day but walk round the room to
show how strong he was.

"Now, my lord, guard the door—take care,"
said Osmond. "You have no loss to-day, for
the King has brought home Herluin of Montreuil, whom you would be almost as loath to
meet as the Fleming. And tell your beads
while I am gone, that the Saints may bring us
out of our peril."

Osmond was absent nearly half an hour,
and when he returned, brought on his shoulders a huge bundle of straw. "What is this
for?" exclaimed Richard. "I wanted my supper, and you have brought straw!"

"Here is your supper," said Osmond, throwing down the straw, and producing a bag with
some bread and meat. "What should you say,
my lord, if we should sup in Normandy to-
morrow night?"

"In Normandy!" cried Richard, springing
up and clapping his hands. "In Normandy!

O Osmond, did you say in Normandy? Shall
we, shall we really? Oh, joy! joy! Is Count
Bernard come? Will the King let us go?"

"Hush! hush, sir—it must be our own doing; it will all fail if you are not silent and
prudent, and we shall be undone."

"I will do anything to get home again!"

"Eat first," said Osmond.

"But what are you going to do? I will not
be as foolish as I was when you tried to get
me safe out of Rollo's Tower. But I should
like to wish Carloman farewell."

"That must not be," said Osmond; "we
should not have time to escape if they did
not still believe you very ill in bed."

"I am sorry not to wish Carloman good-
bye," repeated Richard; "but we shall see
Fru Astrida again and Sir Eric; and Alberic
must come back again! Oh, do let us go!
O Normandy, dear Normandy!"

Richard could hardly eat for excitement,
while Osmond hastily made his arrangements,
girding on his sword, and giving Richard
his dagger to put into his belt. He placed the

remainder of the provisions in his wallet, threw a thick purple cloth mantle over the Duke, and then desired him to lie down on the straw which he had brought in. "I shall hide you in it," he said, "and carry you through the hall, as if I was going to feed my horse."

"Oh, they will never guess!" cried Richard, laughing. "I will be quite still—I will make no noise—I will hold my breath."

"Yes, mind you do not move hand or foot, or rustle the straw. It is no play—it is life or death," said Osmond, as he disposed the straw round the little boy. "There, can you breathe?"

"Yes," said Richard's voice from the midst. "Am I quite hidden?"

"Entirely. Now, remember, whatever happens, do not move! May Heaven protect us! Now the Saints be with us!"

Richard, from the interior of the bundle, heard Osmond set open the door; then he felt himself raised from the ground; Osmond was carrying him along down the stairs, the ends

12

of the straw crushing and sweeping against the wall. The only way to the outer door was through the hall, and here was the danger. Richard heard voices, steps, loud singing and laughter, as if feasting was going on; then some one said, "Tending your horse, Sieur de Centeville?"

"Yes," Osmond made answer. "You know, since we lost our grooms, the poor black would come off badly did I not attend to him."

Presently came Carloman's voice: "O Osmond de Centeville! is Richard better?"

"He is better, my lord, I thank you, but hardly yet out of danger."

"Oh, I wish he was well! And when will you let me come to him, Osmond? Indeed, I would sit quiet and not disturb him."

"It may not be yet, my lord, though the Duke loves you well—he told me so but now."

"Did he? Oh, tell him I love him very much—better than any one here—and it is very dull without him. Tell him so, Osmond."

Richard could hardly help calling out to his

dear little Carloman, but he remembered the peril of Osmond's eyes and the Queen's threat, and held his peace, with some vague notion that some day he would make Carloman King of France. In the meantime, half stifled with straw, he felt himself carried on, down the steps, across the court; and then he knew from the darkness and the changed sound of Osmond's tread, that they were in the stable. Osmond laid him carefully down, and whispered:

"All right, so far. You can breathe?"

"Not well. Can't you let me out?"

"Not yet—not for worlds. Now, tell me if I put you face downwards, for I cannot see."

He laid the living heap of straw across the saddle, bound it on, then led out the horse, gazing round cautiously as he did so; but the whole of the people of the castle were feasting, and there was no one to watch the gates. Richard heard the hollow sound of the hoofs as the drawbridge was crossed, and knew that he was free, but still Osmond held his arm over him, and would not let him move for some distance. Then, just as Richard felt as if he could endure the stifling of the straw and his uncomfortable position not a moment longer, Osmond stopped the horse, took him down, laid him on the grass, and released him. He gazed round—they were in a little wood—evening twilight was just coming on, and the birds sang sweetly.

"Free, free,—this is freedom!" cried Richard, leaping up in the delicious cool evening breeze; "the Queen and Lothaire, and that grim room, all far behind!"

"Not so far yet," said Osmond. "You must not call yourself safe till the Epte is between us and them. Into the saddle, my lord; we must ride for our lives."

Osmond helped the Duke to mount, and sprang to the saddle behind him, set spurs to the horse, and rode on at a quick rate, though not at full speed, as he wished to spare the horse. The twilight faded, the stars came out, and still he rode, his arm round the child, who, as night advanced, grew weary, and often sank into a sort of half doze, conscious all the time of the trot of the horse. But each step was taking him farther from Queen Gerberge and nearer to Normandy, and what recked he of weariness? On—on—the stars grew pale again, and the first pink light of dawn showed in the eastern sky; the sun rose, mounted higher and higher, and the day grew hotter; the horse went more slowly, stumbled, and though Osmond halted and loosed the girth, he only mended his pace for a little while.

Osmond looked grievously perplexed, but they had not gone much farther before a party of merchants came in sight, winding their way with a long train of loaded mules, and stout men to guard them, across the plains, like an Eastern caravan in the desert. They gazed in surprise at the tall young Norman holding the child upon the worn-out warhorse.

"Sir merchant," said Osmond to the first, "see you this steed? Better horse never was ridden, but he is sorely spent, and we must

make speed. Let me barter him with you
for yonder stout palfrey. He is worth twice
as much, but I cannot stop to chaffer—ay or
no at once."

The merchant, seeing the value of Osmond's
gallant black, accepted the offer; and Osmond,
removing his saddle, and placing Richard on
his new steed, again mounted, and on they
went through the country which Osmond's
eye had marked with the sagacity men ac-
quire by living in wild unsettled places. The
great marshes were now far less dangerous
than in the winter, and they safely crossed
them. There had as yet been no pursuit, and
Osmond's only fear was for his little charge,
who, not having recovered his full strength
since his illness, began to suffer greatly from
fatigue in the heat of that broiling summer
day, and leant against Osmond patiently, but
very wearily, without moving or looking up.
He scarcely revived when the sun went down,
and a cool breeze sprang up which much refreshed Osmond himself. And still more did
it refresh the squire to see, at length, wind-

ing through the green pastures, a blue river, on the opposite bank of which rose a high rocky mound, bearing a castle with many a turret and battlement.

"The Epte! the Epte! There is Normandy, sir! Look up, and see your own dukedom."

"Normandy!" cried Richard, sitting upright. "Oh, my own home!"

Still the Epte was wide and deep, and the peril was not yet ended. Osmond looked anxiously, and rejoiced to see marks of cattle, as if it had been forded. "We must try it," he said, and dismounting, he waded in, leading the horse, and firmly holding Richard in the saddle. Deep they went; the water rose to Richard's feet, then to the horse's neck, then the horse was swimming, and Osmond too, still keeping his firm hold; then there was ground again, the force of the current was less, and they were gaining the bank. At that instant, however, they perceived two men aiming at them with crossbows from the castle, and another standing on the bank above them, who called out, "Hold! none pass the ford of Montémar without permission of the noble Dame Yolande."

"Ha! Bertrand the seneschal, is that you?" returned Osmond.

"Who calls me by my name?" replied the seneschal.

"It is I, Osmond de Centeville. Open your gates quickly, Sir Seneschal, for here is the Duke, sorely in need of rest and refreshment."

"The Duke!" exclaimed Bertrand, hurrying down to the landing-place, and throwing off his cap.

"The Duke, the Duke!" rang out the shout from the men-at-arms on the battlements above, and in an instant more Osmond had led the horse up from the water, and was exclaiming, "Look up, my lord, look up! You are in your own dukedom again, and this is Alberic's castle!"

"Welcome, indeed, most noble Lord Duke! Blessings on the day!" cried the seneschal. "What joy for my lady and my young lord!"

"He is sorely weary," said Osmond, looking anxiously at Richard, who, even at the welcome cries that showed so plainly that he was in his own Normandy, scarcely raised himself or spoke. "He had been very sick ere I brought him away. I doubt me they sought to poison him, and I vowed not to tarry at Laon another hour after he was fit to move. But cheer up, my lord, you are safe and free now, and here is the good Dame de Montémar to tend you, far better than a rude squire like me."

"Alas! no," said the seneschal, "our dame is gone with young Alberic on a pilgrimage to Jumièges to pray for the Duke's safety. What joy for them to know that their prayers have been granted!"

Osmond, however, could scarcely rejoice, so alarmed was he at the extreme weariness and exhaustion of his charge, who, when they brought him into the castle hall, hardly spoke or looked, and could not eat. They carried him up to Alberic's bed, where he tossed about restlessly, too tired to sleep.

"Alas! alas!" said Osmond, "I have been too

hasty. I have but saved him from the Franks to be his death by my own imprudence."

"Hush! Sieur de Centeville," said the seneschal's wife, coming into the room; "to talk in that manner is the way to be his death indeed. Leave the child to me—he is only over-weary."

Osmond was sure his Duke was among friends, and would have been glad to trust him to a woman; but Richard had but one instinct left in all his weakness and exhaustion—to cling close to Osmond, as if he felt him his only friend and protector, for he was as yet too much worn out to understand that he was in Normandy and safe. For two or three hours, therefore, Osmond and the seneschal's wife watched on each side of his bed, soothing his restlessness, until at length he became quiet, and at last dropped sound asleep.

The sun was high in the heavens when Richard awoke. He turned on his straw-filled crib and looked up. It was not the tapestried walls of his chamber at Laon that met his opening eyes, but the rugged stone and tall loophole window of a turret chamber. Osmond de Centeville lay on the floor by his side, in the sound sleep of one overcome by long watching and weariness. And what more did Richard see?

It was the bright face and sparkling eyes of Alberic de Montémar, who was leaning against the foot of his bed, gazing earnestly as he watched for his waking. There was a cry, "Alberic! Alberic!" "My lord, my lord!" Richard sat up and held out both arms, and Alberic flung himself into them. They hugged each other, and uttered broken exclamations and screams of joy, enough to have awakened any sleeper but one so wearied out as Osmond.

"And is it true? Oh! am I really in Normandy again?" cried Richard.

"Yes! yes! Oh yes, my lord. You are at Montémar. Everything here is yours. The bar-tailed hawk is quite well, and my mother will be here this evening—she let me ride on the instant we heard the news."

"We rode long and late, and I was very weary," said Richard, "but I don't care, now we are at home. But I can hardly believe it! O Alberic, it has been very dreary."

"See here, my lord!" said Alberic, standing by the window. "Look here, and you will know you are at home again."

Richard bounded to the window, and what a sight met his eyes! The castle court was thronged with men-at-arms and horses, the morning sun sparkling on many a burnished hauberk and tall conical helmet, and above them waved many a banner and pennon that Richard knew full well. "There! there!" he shouted aloud with glee. "Oh, there is the horse-shoe of Ferrières! and there the chequers of Warenne! Oh, and best of all, there is—there is our own red pennon of Centeville! O Alberic! Alberic! is Sir Eric here? I must go down to him!"

"Bertrand sent out notice to them all, as soon as you came, to come and guard our castle," said Alberic, "lest the Franks should pursue you; but you are safe now—safe as Norman spears can make you—thanks be to God!"

"Yes, thanks to God!" said Richard, crossing himself, and kneeling reverently for some minutes, while he repeated his Latin prayer; then, rising and looking at Alberic, he said, "I must thank Him indeed, for He has saved Osmond and me from the cruel King and Queen, and I must try to be a less hasty and overbearing boy than I was when I went away; for I vowed that so I would be, if ever I came back. Poor Osmond, how soundly he sleeps! Come, Alberic, show me the way to Sir Eric!"

And holding Alberic's hand, Richard left the room, and descended the stairs to the castle hall. Many of the Norman knights and barons in full armour were gathered there, but Richard looked for only one; he knew Sir Eric's grizzled hair, and blue inlaid armour, though his back was towards him, and in a moment, before his entrance had been perceived, he sprang towards him, and with outstretched arms, exclaimed, "Sir Eric, dear Sir Eric, here I am! Osmond is safe! and is Fru Astrida well?"

The old Baron turned. "My child!" he exclaimed, and clasped him in his mailed arms, while the tears flowed down his rugged cheeks. "Blessed be God that you are safe, and that my son has done his duty!"

"And is Fru Astrida well?"

"Yes, right well, since she heard of your safety. But look round, my lord; it befits not a duke to be clinging thus round an old man's neck. See how many of your true vassals be here to guard you from the villain Franks."

Richard stood up, and held out his hand, bowing courteously, and acknowledging the greeting of each bold Baron, with a grace and readiness he certainly had not when he left Normandy. He was taller too, and though still pale, and not dressed with much care (since he had hurried on his clothes with no help but Alberic's), though his hair was rough and disordered, and the scar of the burn had not yet faded from his cheek—yet still, with his bright blue eyes, glad face, and upright form, he was a princely, promising boy, and the Norman knights looked at him with pride and joy, more especially when, unprompted, he said, "I thank you, gallant knights, for coming to guard me. I do not fear the whole French host, now I am among my own true Normans."

Sir Eric led him to the door of the hall at the top of the steps, that the men-at-arms might see him, and then such a shout rang out of "Long live Duke Richard! Blessings on the little Duke," that it echoed, and came back again from the hills around—it pealed from the old tower—it roused Osmond from his sleep, and if anything more had been wanting to do so, it made Richard feel that he was indeed in a land where every heart glowed with loyal love for him.

Before the shout had died away, a bugle-horn was heard winding before the gate, and Sir Eric, saying, "It is the Count of Harcourt's note," sent Bertrand to open the gates in haste, while Alberic followed, as lord of the castle, to receive the Count.

The old Count rode into the court, and to the foot of the steps, where he dismounted, Alberic holding his stirrup. He had not taken many steps upwards before Richard came voluntarily to meet him (which he had never done before), held out his hand, and said, "Welcome, Count Bernard, welcome! Thank you for coming to guard me. I am very glad to see you once more."

"Ah! my young lord," said Bernard, "I am right glad to see you out of the clutches of the Franks. You know friend from foe now, methinks!"

"Yes, indeed I do, Count Bernard. I know you meant kindly by me, and that I ought to have thanked you, and not been angry when you reproved me. Wait one moment, Sir Count; there is one thing that I promised myself to say, if ever I came safe to my own

Richard made but one bound into her arms.

dear home.   Walter,—Maurice,—Jeannot,—
all you of my household, and of Sir Eric's—
I know before I went away I was often no
good lord to you. I was passionate, and
proud, and overbearing; but God has punished
me for it, when I was far away among my
enemies, and sick and lonely. I am very sorry
for it, and I hope you will pardon me, for I
will strive, and I hope God will help me, never
to be proud and passionate again."

"There, Sir Eric," said Bernard, "you hear
what the boy says. If he speaks it out so bold
and free, without bidding, and if he holds to
what he says, I doubt it not that he shall not
grieve for his journey to France, and that we
shall see him, in all things, such a Prince as
his father of blessed memory."

"You must thank Osmond for me," said
Richard, as Osmond came down, awakened
at length. "It is Osmond who has helped me
to bear my troubles; and as to saving me—
why, he flew away with me even like an old
eagle with its eaglet. I say, Osmond, you
must ever after this wear a pair of wings

on shield and pennon, to show how well we managed our flight." [1]

"As you will, my lord," said Osmond, half asleep; "but 'twas a good long flight at a stretch, and I trust never to have to fly before your foes or mine again."

What a glad summer's-day was that! Even the three hours spent in council did but renew the relish with which Richard visited Alberic's treasures, told his adventures, and showed the accomplishments he had learnt at Laon. The evening was more joyous still, for the castle gates were opened, first to receive Dame Yolande de Montémar, and not above a quarter of an hour afterwards, the draw-bridge was lowered to admit the followers of Centeville, and in front of them appeared Fru Astrida's own high cap. Richard made but one bound into her arms, and was clasped to

[1] "Gules, two wings conjoined in lure, or," is the original coat of St. Maur or Seymour, said to be derived from Osmond de Centeville, who assumed them in honour of his flight with Duke Richard. His direct descendants in Normandy were the Marquises of Osmond, whose arms were, gules, two wings ermine. In 1789, there were two survivors of the line of Centeville, one a canon of Notre Dame, the other a Chevalier de St. Louis, who died childless.

her breast, then held off at arms' length, that she might see how much he was grown, and pity his scar, then hugged closer than ever! but taking another look, she declared that Osmond left his hair like King Harald Horridlocks;[1] and drawing an ivory comb from her pouch, began to pull out the thick tangles, hurting him to a degree that would once have made him rebel, but now he only fondled her the more.

As to Osmond, when he knelt before her, she blessed him and sobbed over him, and blamed him for over-tiring her darling, all in one; and assuredly when night closed in, and Richard had, as of old, told his beads beside her knee, the happiest boy in Normandy was its little Duke.

[1] Harald of Norway, who made a vow never to trim his hair till he had made himself sole king of the country. The war lasted ten years, and he thus might well come to deserve his title of Horridlocks, which was changed to that of Harfagre, or fair-haired, when he celebrated his final victory, by going into a bath at Möre, and committing his shaggy hair to be cut and arranged by his friend, Jarl Rognwald, father of Rollo.

CHAPTER IX

Montémar was too near the frontier to be a safe abode for the little Duke, and his uncle, Count Hubert of Senlis, agreed with Bernard the Dane that he would be more secure beyond the limits of his own duchy, which was likely soon to be the scene of war; and, sorely against his will, he was sent in secret, under a strong escort, first to the castle of Coucy, and afterwards to Senlis.

His consolation was that he was not again separated from his friends; Alberic, Sir Eric, and even Fru Astrida accompanied him, as well as his constant follower, Osmond. Indeed, the Baron would hardly bear that he should be out of his sight; and he was still so carefully watched, that it was almost like captivity. Never, even in the summer days, was he allowed to go beyond the castle walls, and his guardians would fain have had it supposed that the castle did not contain any such guest.

197

Osmond did not give him so much of his company as usual, but was always at work in the armourer's forge—a low vaulted chamber, opening into the castle court. Richard and Alberic were very curious to know what he did there; but he fastened the door with an iron bar, and they were forced to content themselves with listening to the strokes of the hammer keeping time to the voices that sang out, loud and cheerily, the song of "Sigurd's sword, and the maiden sleeping within the ring of flame." Fru Astrida said Osmond was quite right—no good weapon-smith ever toiled with open doors, and when the boys asked him questions as to his work, he only smiled and said that they should see what it was when the call to arms should come.

They thought it near at hand, for tidings came that Louis had assembled his army, and marched into Normandy to recover the person of the young Duke, and to seize the country. No summons, however, arrived, but a message came instead, that Rouen had been surrendered into the hands of the King. Richard shed indignant tears. "My father's castle! My own city in the hands of the foe! Bernard is a traitor then! None shall hinder me from so calling him. Why did we trust him?"

"Never fear, Lord Duke," said Osmond. "When you come to the years of knighthood, your own sword shall right you, in spite of all the false Danes and falser Franks in the land."

"What! you too, son Osmond? I deemed you carried a cooler brain than to miscall one who was true to Rollo's race before you or yon varlet were born!" said the old Baron.

"He has yielded my dukedom! It is miscalling to say he is aught but a traitor!" cried Richard. "Vile, treacherous, favour-seeking——"

"Peace, peace, my lord," said the Baron. "Bernard has more in that wary head of his than your young wits, or my old ones, can unwind. What he is doing, I may not guess, but I gage my life his heart is right."

Richard was silent, remembering he had been once unjust, but he grieved heartily when he thought of the French in Rollo's Tower, and it was further reported that the King was about to share Normandy among his French vassals. A fresh outcry broke out in the little garrison of Senlis, but Sir Eric still persisted in his trust in his friend Bernard, even when he heard that Centeville was marked out as the prey of the fat French count who had served for a hostage at Rouen.

"What say you now, my lord?" said he, after a conference with a messenger at the gate. "The *Black Raven* has spread its wings. Fifty keels are in the Seine, and Harald Blue-tooth's Long Serpent at the head of them."

"The King of Denmark! Come to my aid?"

"Ay, that he is! Come at Bernard's secret call to right you, and put you on your father's seat. Now call honest Harcourt a traitor because he gave not up your fair dukedom to the flame and the sword."

"No traitor to me," said Richard, pausing.

"No, verily, but what more would you say?"

"I think when I come to my dukedom, I will not be so politic," said Richard. "I will be an open friend or an open foe."

"The boy grows too sharp for us," said Sir Eric, smiling, "but it was spoken like his father."

"He grows more like his blessed father each day," said Fru Astrida.

"But the Danes, father, the Danes!" said Osmond. "Blows will be passing now. I may join the host and win my spurs?"

"With all my heart," returned the Baron, "so my lord here gives you leave; would that I could leave him and go with you. It would do my very spirit good but to set foot in a Northern keel once more."

"I would fain see what these men of the North are," said Osmond.

"Oh! they are only Danes, not Norsemen, and there are no Vikings, such as once were when Ragnar laid waste——"

"Son, son, what talk is this for the child's ears?" broke in Fru Astrida; "are these words for a Christian Baron?"

"Your pardon, mother," said the grey warrior in all humility, "but my blood thrills to hear of a Northern fleet at hand, and to think of Osmond drawing sword under a sea-king."

The next morning Osmond's steed was led to the door, and such men-at-arms as could be spared from the garrison of Senlis were drawn up in readiness to accompany him. The boys stood on the steps, wishing they were old enough to be warriors, and wondering what had become of him, until at length the sound of an opening door startled them, and there, in the low archway of the smithy, the red furnace glowing behind him, stood Osmond, clad in bright steel, the links of his hauberk reflecting the light, and on his helmet a pair of golden wings, while the same device adorned his long pointed kite-shaped shield.

"Your wings! our wings!" cried Richard, "the bearing of Centeville!"

"May they fly after the foe, not before him,"

said Sir Eric. "Speed thee well, my son; let not our Danish cousins say we learn Frank graces instead of Northern blows."

With such farewells Osmond quitted Senlis, while the two boys hastened to the battlements to watch him as long as he remained in view.

The highest tower became their principal resort, and their eyes were constantly on the heath where he had disappeared; but days passed, and they grew weary of the watch, and betook themselves to games in the castle court.

One day Alberic, in the character of a dragon, was lying on his back, panting hard so as to be supposed to cast out volumes of flame and smoke at Richard, the Knight, who with a stick for a lance, and a wooden sword, was waging fierce war; when suddenly the dragon paused, sat up, and pointed towards the warder on the tower. His horn was at his lips, and in another moment the blast rang out through the castle.

With a loud shout both boys rushed head-

ered around him asking hurried questions.
A great victory—the King a prisoner—
Montreuil slain!

Richard would not be denied holding his
hand, and leading him to the hall; and there,
sitting around him, they heard his tidings.
His father's first question was what he
thought of their kinsmen, the Danes?

"Rude comrades, father, I must own," said
Osmond, smiling and shaking his head. "I
could not pledge them in a skull-goblet—set
in gold though it were."

"None the worse warriors," said Sir Eric.
"Ay, ay, and you were dainty, and brooked
not the hearty old fashion of tearing the
whole sheep to pieces. You must needs cut
your portion with the fine French knife at
your girdle."

Osmond could not see that a man was
braver for being a savage, but he held his
peace; and Richard impatiently begged to
hear how the battle had gone, and where it
had been fought.

"On the bank of the Dive," said Osmond.

"Ah, father, you might well call old Harcourt wary—his name might better have been Fox-heart than Bear-heart! He had sent to the Franks a message of distress, that the Danes were on him in full force, and to pray them to come to his aid."

"I trust there was no treachery. No foul dealing shall be wrought in my name!" exclaimed Richard, with such dignity of tone and manner as made all feel he was indeed their Duke, and forget his tender years.

"No, or should I tell the tale with joy like this?" said Osmond. "Bernard's view was to bring the Kings together, and let Louis see you had friends to maintain your right. He sought but to avoid bloodshed."

"And how chanced it?"

"The Danes were encamped on the Dive, and so soon as the French came in sight, Blue-tooth sent a messenger to Louis to summon him to quit Neustria, and leave it to you, its lawful owner. Thereupon Louis, hoping to win him over with wily words, invited him to hold a personal conference."

"Where were you, Osmond?"

"Where I had scarce patience to be. Bernard had gathered all of us honest Normans together, and arranged us beneath that standard of the King, as if to repel this Danish inroad. Oh! he was in all seeming hand-and-glove with Louis, guiding him by his counsel, and, verily, seeming his friend and best adviser. But in one thing he could not prevail; that ungrateful recreant Herluin of Montreuil came with the King, hoping, it seems, to get his share of our spoils; and when Bernard advised the King to send him home, since no true Norman could bear the sight of him, the hot-headed Franks vowed no Norman should hinder them from bringing whom they chose. So a tent was set up by the river side, wherein the two kings, with Bernard, Alan of Brittany, and Count Hugh, held their meeting. We all stood without, and the two hosts began to mingle together, we Normans making acquaintance with the Danes. There was a red-haired wild-looking fellow, who told me he had been with Anlaff in England,

and spoke much of the doings of Hako in Norway, when suddenly he pointed to a knight who was near, speaking to a Cotentinois, and asked me his name. My blood boiled as I answered, for it was Montreuil himself! 'The cause of your Duke's death!' said the Dane. 'Ha, ye Normans are fallen sons of Odin to see him yet live!' "

"You said, I trust, my son, that we follow not the laws of Odin?" said Fru Astrida.

"I had no space for a word, grandmother; the Danes took the vengeance on themselves. In one moment they rushed on Herluin with their axes, and the unhappy man was dead. All was tumult. Every one struck without knowing at whom or for what. Some shouted 'Thor Hulf,' some 'Dieu aide,' others 'Montjoie St. Denis.' Northern blood against French—that was all our guide. I found myself at the foot of this standard, and had a hard combat for it, but I bore it away at last."

"And the kings?"

"They hurried out of the tent, it seems, to rejoin their men. Louis mounted, but you

14

know of old, my lord, he is but an indifferent horseman, and the beast carried him into the midst of the Danes, where King Harald caught his bridle, and delivered him to four knights to keep. Whether he dealt secretly with them, or whether they, as they declared, lost sight of him whilst plundering his tent, I cannot say; but when Harald demanded him of them he was gone!"

"Gone! is this what you call having the King prisoner?"

"You shall hear. He rode four leagues, and met one of the baser sort of Rouennais, whom he bribed to hide him in the Isle of Willows. However, Bernard made close inquiries, found the fellow had been seen in speech with a French horseman, pounced on his wife and children, and threatened they should die if he did not disclose the secret. So the King was forced to come out of his hiding-place, and is now fast guarded in Rollo's Tower—a Dane with a battle-axe on his shoulder keeping guard at every turn of the stairs."

"Ha! ha!" cried Richard. "I wonder how

he likes it. I wonder if he remembers holding me up to the window, and vowing that he meant me only good!"

"When you believed him, my lord," said Osmond slyly.

"I was a little boy then," said Richard proudly. "Why, the very walls must remind him of his oath, and how Count Bernard said, as he dealt with me so might Heaven deal with him."

"Remember it, my child—beware of broken vows," said Father Lucas; "but remember it not in triumph over a fallen foe. It were better that all came at once to the chapel, to bestow their thanksgivings where alone they are due."

CHAPTER X

After nearly a year's captivity, the King engaged to pay a ransom, and, until the terms could be arranged, his two sons were to be placed as hostages in the hands of the Normans, whilst he returned to his own domains. The Princes were to be sent to Bayeux, whither Richard had returned, under the charge of the Centevilles, and was now allowed to ride and walk abroad freely, provided he was accompanied by a guard.

"I shall rejoice to have Carloman and make him happy," said Richard; "but I wish Lothaire were not coming."

"Perhaps," said good Father Lucas, "he comes that you may have a first trial in your father's last lesson, and Abbot Martin's, and return good for evil."

The Duke's cheek flushed, and he made no answer.

He and Alberic betook themselves to the watch-tower, and, by-and-by, saw a cavalcade approaching, with a curtained vehicle in the midst, slung between two horses. "That cannot be the Princes," said Alberic; "that must surely be some sick lady."

"I only hope it is not the Queen," exclaimed Richard in dismay. "But no, Lothaire is such a coward, no doubt he was afraid to ride, and she would not trust her darling, without shutting him up like a demoiselle. But come down, Alberic; I will say nothing unkind of Lothaire, if I can help it."

Richard met the Princes in the court, his sunny hair uncovered, and bowing with such becoming courtesy that Fru Astrida pressed her son's arm, and bade him say if their little Duke was not the fairest and noblest child in Christendom.

With black looks, Lothaire stepped from the litter, took no heed of the little Duke, but roughly calling his attendant Charlot to follow him, he marched into the hall, vouchsafing neither word nor look to any as he passed, threw himself into the highest seat, and ordered Charlot to bring him some wine.

Meanwhile, Richard, looking into the litter, saw Carloman crouching in a corner, sobbing with fright.

"Carloman, dear Carloman, do not cry! Come out—it is I, your own Richard. Will you not let me welcome you?"

Carloman looked up, caught at the outstretched hand, and clung to his neck.

"O Richard, send us back, do not let the savage Danes kill us."

"No one will hurt you. There are no Danes here; you are my guest, my friend, my brother. Look up—here is my own Fru Astrida."

"But my mother said the Northmen would kill us for keeping you captive. She wept and raved, and the cruel men dragged us away by force. Oh, let us go back!"

"I cannot do that," said Richard, "for you are the King of Denmark's captives, not mine; but I will love you, and you shall have all that is mine, if you will only not cry, dear Carloman. Oh, Fru Astrida, what shall I do? You comfort him——" as the poor boy clung sobbing to him.

Fru Astrida advanced to take his hand, speaking in a soothing voice, but he shrank and started with a fresh cry of terror—her tall figure, high cap, and wrinkled face were to him witch-like, and as she knew no French, he understood not her kind words. However, he let Richard lead him into the hall, where Lothaire sat moodily in the chair, with one leg tucked under him, and his finger in his mouth.

"I say, Sir Duke," said he, "is there nothing to be had in this old den of yours? Not a drop of Bordeaux?"

Richard tried to repress his anger at this uncivil way of speaking, and answered, that he thought there was none, but there was plenty of Norman cider.

"As if I would taste your mean peasant drinks! I bade them bring my supper; why does it not come?"

"Because you are not master here," trembled on Richard's lips; but he forced it back, and answered that it would soon be ready, and Carloman looked imploringly at his brother and said, "Do not make them angry, Lothaire."

"What, crying still, foolish child?" said
Lothaire. "Do you not know that if they dare
to cross us, my father will treat them as they
deserve? Bring supper, and let me have a
pasty of ortolans."

"There are none—they are not in season,"
said Richard.

"Do you mean to give me nothing I like? I
tell you it shall be the worse for you."

"There is a pullet roasting," began Richard.

"I tell you, I do not care for pullets; I will
have ortolans."

"If I do not take order with that boy, my
name is not Eric," muttered the Baron.

"What must he not have made our poor
child suffer!" returned Fru Astrida; "but the
little one moves my heart. How small and
weakly he is; but it is worth anything to see
our little Duke so tender to him."

"He is too brave not to be gentle," said Osmond; and, indeed, the high-spirited impetu-
ous boy was as soft and kind as a maiden with
that feeble, timid child. He coaxed him to eat,
consoled him, and, instead of laughing at his

fears, kept between him and the great blood-hound, Hardigras, and drove it off when it came too near.

"Take that dog away," said Lothaire imperiously. No one moved to obey him, and the dog, in seeking for scraps, again came towards him.

"Take it away," he repeated, and struck it with his foot. The dog growled, and Richard started up in indignation.

"Prince Lothaire," he said, "I care not what else you do, but my dogs and my people you shall not maltreat."

"I tell you I am Prince! I do what I will! Ha! who laughs there?" cried the passionate boy, stamping on the floor.

"It is not so easy for French princes to scourge freeborn Normans here," said the rough voice of Walter the huntsman; "there is a reckoning for the stripe my Lord Duke bore for me."

"Hush, hush, Walter," began Richard; but Lothaire had caught up a footstool, and was aiming it at the huntsman, when his arm was

caught. Osmond, who knew him well enough
to be prepared for some such outbreak, held
him fast by both hands, in spite of his passionate screams and struggles, which were like
those of one frantic.

Sir Eric, meanwhile, thundered forth in his
Norman patois, "I would have you to know,
young sir, Prince though you be, you are our
prisoner, and shall taste of a dungeon, and
bread and water, unless you behave yourself."

Either Lothaire did not hear, or did not believe, and fought more furiously in Osmond's
arms, but he had little chance with the stalwart young warrior, and, in spite of Richard's
remonstrances, he was carried from the hall,
roaring and kicking, and locked up alone in
an empty room.

"Let him alone for the present," said Sir
Eric, putting the Duke aside; "when he knows
his master, we shall have peace."

Here Richard had to turn to reassure Carloman, who had taken refuge in a dark corner,
and there shook like an aspen leaf, crying

Lothaire had caught up a footstool,

bitterly, and starting with fright when Richard touched him.

"Oh, do not put me in the dungeon! I cannot bear the dark."

Richard again tried to comfort him, but he did not seem to hear or heed. "Oh! they said you would beat and hurt us for what we did to you! but, indeed, it was not I that burnt your cheek!"

"We would not hurt you for worlds, dear Carloman; Lothaire is not in the dungeon— he is only shut up till he is good."

"It was Lothaire that did it," repeated Carloman, "and, indeed, you must not be angry with me, for my mother was so cross with me for not having stopped Osmond when I met him with the bundle of straw, that she gave me a blow that knocked me down. And were you really there, Richard?"

Richard told his story, and was glad to find Carloman could smile at it; and then Fru Astrida advised him to take his little friend to bed. Carloman would not lie down without still holding Richard's hand, and the little

Duke spared no pains to set him at rest, knowing what it was to be a desolate captive far from home.

"I thought you would be good to me," said Carloman. "As to Lothaire, it serves him right that you should use him as he used you."

"Oh no, Carloman; if I had a brother, I would never speak so of him."

"But Lothaire is so unkind."

"Ah! but we must be kind to those who are unkind to us."

The child rose on his elbow, and looked into Richard's face. "No one ever told me so before."

"O Carloman, not Brother Hilary?"

"I never heed Brother Hilary—he is so lengthy, and wearisome; besides, no one is ever kind to those that hate them."

"My father was," said Richard.

"And they killed him!" said Carloman.

"Yes," said Richard, crossing himself, "but he is gone to be in peace."

"I wonder if it is happier there than here,"

said Carloman. "I am not happy. But tell me, why should we be good to those that hate us?"

"Because the Holy Saints were. And look at the Crucifix, Carloman; that was for them that hated Him. And don't you know what our Pater Noster says?"

Poor little Carloman could only repeat the Lord's Prayer in Latin—he had not the least notion of its meaning, in which Richard had been carefully instructed by Father Lucas. He began to explain it, but before many words had passed his lips, little Carloman was asleep.

The Duke crept softly away to beg to be allowed to go to Lothaire; he entered the room, already dark, with a pine torch in his hand, that so flickered in the wind, that he could at first see nothing, but presently beheld a dark lump on the floor.

"Prince Lothaire," he said, "here is——"

Lothaire cut him short. "Get away," he said. "If it is your turn now, it will be mine by-and-by. I wish my mother had kept her word, and put your eyes out."

Richard's temper did not serve for such a

reply. "It is a foul shame of you to speak so, when I only came out of kindness to you, so I shall leave you here all night, and not ask Sir Eric to let you out."

And he swung back the heavy door with a resounding clang. But his heart smote him when he told his beads, and remembered what he had said to Carloman. He knew he could not sleep in his warm bed when Lothaire was in that cold gusty room. To be sure, Sir Eric said it would do him good, but Sir Eric little knew how tender the French Princes were.

So Richard crept down in the dark, slid back the bolt, and called, "Prince, Prince, I am sorry I was angry. Come out, and let us try to be friends."

"What do you mean?" said Lothaire.

"Come out of the cold and dark. Here am I. I will show you the way. Where is your hand? Oh, how cold it is! Let me lead you down to the hall fire."

Lothaire was subdued by fright, cold, and darkness, and quietly allowed Richard to lead him down. Round the fire, at the lower end of

the hall, snored half-a-dozen men-at-arms; at
the upper hearth there was only Hardigras,
who raised his head as the boys came in.
Richard's whisper and soft pat quieted him
instantly, and the two little Princes sat on the
hearth together, Lothaire surprised, but
sullen. Richard stirred the embers so as to
bring out more heat, then spoke: "Prince, will
you let us be friends?"

"I must, if I am in your power."

"I wish you would be my guest and comrade."

"Well, I will; I can't help it."

Richard thought his advances might have
been more graciously met, and, having little
encouragement to say more, took Lothaire to
bed as soon as he was warm.

CHAPTER XI

As the Baron had said, there was more peace
now that Lothaire had learnt to know that he
must submit, and that no one cared for his
threats of his father's or his mother's vengeance. He was very sulky and disagreeable,
and severely tried Richard's forbearance; but
there were no fresh outbursts, and on the
whole, from one week to another, there might
be said to be an improvement. He could not
always hold aloof from one so good-natured
and good-humoured as the little Duke; and
the fact of being kept in order could not but
have some beneficial effect on him, after such
spoiling as his had been at home.

Indeed, Osmond was once heard to say, it
was a pity the boy was not to be a hostage for
life; to which Sir Eric replied, "So long as we
have not the training of him."

Little Carloman, meanwhile, recovered from
his fears of all the inmates of the castle ex-

cepting Hardigras, at whose approach he always shrank and trembled.

He renewed his friendship with Osmond, no longer started at the entrance of Sir Eric, laughed at Alberic's merry ways, and liked to sit on Fru Astrida's lap and hear her sing, though he understood not one word; but his especial love was still for his first friend, Duke Richard. Hand in hand they went about together; Richard sometimes lifting him up the steep steps, and, out of consideration for him, refraining from rough play; and Richard led him to join with him in those lessons that Father Lucas gave the children of the castle every Friday and Sunday evening in the chapel. The good priest stood on the altar steps, with the children in a half-circle round him—the son and daughter of the armourer, the huntsman's little son, the young Baron de Montémar, the Duke of Normandy, and the Prince of France—all were equal there, and together they learnt, as he explained to them the things most needful to believe. And thus Carloman left off wondering why Richard thought it right to be good to his enemies; and though at first he had known less than even the little leather-coated huntsman, he seemed to take the holy lessons in faster than any of them—yes, and to act upon them too. His feeble health seemed to make him enter into their comfort and meaning more than even Richard and Alberic, and Father Lucas soon told Fru Astrida that it was a saintly-minded child.

Indeed, Carloman was the more disposed to thoughtfulness because he was incapable of joining in the sports of the other boys. A race round the court was beyond his strength, the fresh wind on the battlements made him shiver and cower, and loud shouting play was dreadful to him. In old times, he used to cry when Lothaire told him he must have his hair cut and be a priest; now, he only said quietly he should like it very much if he could be good enough.

Fru Astrida sighed, and shook her head, and feared the poor child would never grow up to be anything on this earth. Great as had

been the difference at first between him and
Richard, it was now far greater. Richard was
an unusually strong boy for ten years old, upright and broad-chested, and growing very
fast; while Carloman seemed to dwindle,
stooped forward from weakness, had thin
pinched features and sallow cheeks, looking
like a plant kept in the dark.

The old Baron said that hardy healthy
habits would restore the puny children, and
Lothaire improved in health, and therewith
in temper; but his little brother had not
strength enough to bear the seasoning. He
pined and drooped more each day, and as the
autumn came on, and the wind was chilly, he
grew worse, and was scarcely ever off the lap
of the kind Lady Astrida. It was not a settled
sickness, but he grew weaker, and wasted
away. They made up a little couch for him by
the fire, with a high settle between it and the
door, to keep off the draughts; and there he
used patiently to lie, hour after hour, speaking
feebly, or smiling and seeming pleased when
any one of those he loved approached. He

liked Father Lucas to come and say prayers
with him, and he never failed to have a glad
look when his dear little Duke came to talk to
him in his cheerful voice, about his rides, and
his hunting and hawking adventures. Richard's sick guest took up much of his thoughts,
and he never willingly spent many hours at a
distance from him, softening his step and low-
ering his voice, as he entered the hall, lest
Carloman should be asleep.

"Richard, is it you?" said the little boy, as
the young figure came round the settle in the
darkening twilight.

"Yes. How do you feel now, Carloman, are
you better?"

"No better, thanks, dear Richard," and the
little wasted fingers were put into his.

"Has the pain come again?"

"No, I have been lying still, musing;
Richard, I shall never be better."

"Oh, do not say so! You will, indeed you
will, when spring comes."

"I feel as if I should die," said the little boy.
"I think I shall, but do not grieve, Richard. I

do not feel much afraid. You said it was happier there than here, and I know it now."

"Where my blessed father is," said Richard thoughtfully. "But, O Carloman, you are so young to die."

"I do not want to live. This is a fighting hard world, full of cruel people, and it is peace there. You are strong and brave, and will make them better; but I am weak and fearful—I could only sigh and grieve."

"O Carloman! Carloman! I cannot spare you. I love you like my own brother. You must not die—you must live to see your father and mother again!"

"Commend me to them," said Carloman. "I am going to my Father in heaven. I am glad I am here, Richard; I never was so happy before. I should have been afraid indeed to die, if Father Lucas had not taught me how my sins are pardoned. Now, I think the Saints and angels are waiting for me."

He spoke feebly, and his last words faltered into sleep. He slept on, and when supper was brought, and the lamps were lighted, Fru Astrida thought the little face looked unusually pale and waxen, but he did not awake. At night they carried him to his bed, and he was roused into a half-conscious state, moaning at being disturbed. Fru Astrida would not leave him, and Father Lucas shared her watch.

At midnight, all were wakened by the slow notes, falling one by one on the ear, of the solemn passing-bell, calling them to awaken that their prayers might speed a soul on its way. Richard and Lothaire were soon at the bedside. Carloman still lay asleep, his hands folded on his breast, but his breath came in long gasps. Father Lucas was praying over him, and candles were placed on each side of the bed. All was still, the boys not daring to speak or move. There came a longer breath— then they heard no more. He was indeed gone to a happier home, a truer royalty than ever had been his on earth.

Then the boys' grief burst out. Lothaire screamed for his mother, and sobbed out that he should die too—he must go home. Richard stood by the bed, large silent tears rolling down his cheeks, and his chest heaving with suppressed sobs.

Fru Astrida led them from the room, back to their beds. Lothaire soon cried himself to sleep; Richard lay awake, sorrowful and in deep thought, while that scene in St. Mary's at Rouen returned before his eyes, and though it had passed nearly two years ago, its meaning and its teaching had sunk deep into his mind and now stood before him more completely.

"Where shall I go, when I come to die, if I have not returned good for evil?" And a resolution was taken in the mind of the little Duke.

Morning came, and brought back the sense that his gentle little companion was gone from him; and Richard wept again, as if he could not be consoled, as he beheld the screened couch where the patient smile would never again greet him. He now knew that he had loved Carloman all the more for his weakness and helplessness; but his grief was not like Lothaire's, for with the Prince's, was still joined a selfish fear; his cry was still that he should die too, if not set free, and violent weeping really made him heavy and ill.

The little corpse, embalmed, and lapped in lead, was to be sent back to France, that it might rest with its forefathers in the city of Rheims; and Lothaire seemed to feel this as an additional stroke of desertion. He was almost beside himself with despair, imploring every one, in turn, to send him home, though he well knew they were unable to do so.

CHAPTER XII

"Sir Eric," said Richard, "you told me there was a *Parlement* to be held at Falaise, between Count Bernard and the King of Denmark. I mean to attend it. Will you come with me, or shall Osmond go, and you remain in charge of the Prince?"

"How now, Lord Richard? You were not wont to love a *Parlement*."

"I have something to say," replied Richard. The Baron made no objection, only telling his mother that the Duke was a marvellous wise child, and that he would soon be fit to take the government himself.

Lothaire lamented the more when he found that Richard was going away; his presence seemed to him a protection, and he fancied, now Carloman was dead, that his former injuries were about to be revenged. The Duke assured him repeatedly that he meant him nothing but kindness, adding, "When I return, you will see, Lothaire;" then commending him to the care and kindness of Fru Astrida, Osmond, and Alberic, Richard set forth upon his pony, attended by Sir Eric and three men-at-arms.

Richard felt sad when he looked back at Bayeux, and thought that it no longer contained his dear little friend; but it was a fresh bright frosty morning, the fields were covered with a silvery-white coating, the flakes of hoar-frost sparkled on every bush, and the hard ground rung cheerily to the tread of the horses' feet. As the yellow sun fought his way through the grey mists that dimmed his brightness, and shone out merrily in the blue heights of the sky, Richard's spirits rose, and he laughed and shouted as hare or rabbit rushed across the heath, or as the plover rose screaming above his head, flapping her broad wings across the wintry sky.

One night they slept at a convent, where they heard that Hugh of Paris had passed on to join the conference at Falaise. The next day they rode on, and, towards the afternoon, the Baron pointed to a sharp rocky range of hills, crowned by a tall solid tower, and told Richard yonder was his keep of Falaise, the strongest castle in Normandy.

The country was far more broken as they advanced; narrow valleys, and sharp hills, each little vale full of wood and interspersed with rocks. "A choice place for game," Sir Eric said; and Richard, as he saw a herd of deer dash down a forest glade, exclaimed that they must come here to stay for some autumn sport.

There seemed to be huntsmen abroad in the woods, for through the frosty air came the baying of dogs, the shouts and calls of men, and, now and then, the echoing ringing notes of a bugle. Richard's eyes and cheeks glowed with excitement, and he pushed his brisk little pony on faster and faster, unheeding that the heavier men and horses of his suite were not keeping pace with him on the rough ground and through the tangled boughs.

Presently, a strange sound of growling and snarling was heard close at hand; his pony swerved aside, and could not be made to advance; so Richard, dismounting, dashed through some briars, and there, on an open space, beneath a precipice of dark ivy-covered rock that rose like a wall, he beheld a huge grey wolf and a large dog in mortal combat. It was as if they had fallen or rolled down the precipice together, not heeding it in their fury. Both were bleeding, and the eyes of both glared like red fiery glass in the dark shadow of the rock. The dog lay undermost, almost overpowered, making but a feeble resistance; and the wolf would, in another moment, be at liberty to spring on the lonely child!

But not a thought of fear passed through his breast; to save the dog was Richard's only idea. In one moment he had drawn the dagger he wore at his girdle, ran to the two struggling animals, and with all his force plunged it into the throat of the wolf, which happily was still held by the teeth of the hound.

The struggles relaxed, the wolf rolled heavily aside, dead; the dog lay panting and bleeding, and Richard feared he was cruelly torn. "Poor fellow, noble dog, what shall I do to help you?" and he gently smoothed the dark brindled head.

A voice was now heard shouting aloud, at which the dog raised and crested his head, as a figure in a hunting-dress was coming down a rocky pathway, an extremely tall, well-made man of noble features. "Ha! holla! Vige! Vige! How now, my brave hound?" he said in the Northern tongue, though not quite with the accent Richard was accustomed to hear. "Art hurt?"

"Much torn, I fear," Richard called out, as the faithful creature wagged his tail, and strove to rise and meet his master.

"Ha, lad! what art thou?" exclaimed the hunter, amazed at seeing the boy between the dead wolf and wounded dog. "You look like one of those Frenchified Norman gentilesse, with your smooth locks and gilded baldrick, yet your words are Norse. By the hammer of Thor! that is a dagger in the wolf's throat."

"It is mine," said Richard. "I found your dog nearly spent, and I made in to the rescue."

"You did? Well done! I would not have lost Vige for all the plunder of Italy. I am beholden to you, my brave young lad," said the stranger, all the time examining and caressing the hound. "What is your name? you cannot be southern bred."

As he spoke, more shouts came near, and the Baron de Centeville rushed through the trees, holding Richard's pony by the bridle. "My lord, my lord! Oh, thank Heaven, I see you safe!"

At the same moment a party of hunters also approached by the path, and at the head of them Bernard the Dane. "Ha!" exclaimed he, "what do I see? My young lord! what brought you here?" And with a hasty obeisance, Bernard took Richard's outstretched hand.

"I came hither to attend your council," replied Richard. "I have a boon to ask of the King of Denmark."

"Any boon the King of Denmark has in his power will be yours," said the dog's master, slapping his hand on the little Duke's shoulder,

with a rude, hearty familiarity that took him
by surprise; and he looked up with a shade of
offence, till, on a sudden flash of perception,
he took off his cap, exclaiming, "King Harald
himself! pardon me, Sir King."

"Pardon, Jarl Richard? what would you
have me pardon? your saving the life of Vige,
here? No French politeness for me. Tell me
your boon, and it is yours. Shall I take you a
voyage, and harry the fat monks of Ire-
land?"

Richard recoiled a little from his new
friend.

"Oh, ha! I forgot. They have made a
Christian of you—more's the pity. You have
the Northern spirit so strong, I had forgotten
it. Come, walk by my side, and let me hear
what you would ask. Holla! you Sweyn, carry
Vige up to the castle, and look to his wounds.
Now for it, young Jarl."

"My boon is that you would set free Prince
Lothaire."

"What? the young Frank? Why, they kept
you captive, burnt your face, and would have

made an end of you but for your clever bonder."

"That is long past, and Lothaire is so wretched. His brother is dead, and he is sick with grief, and he says he shall die if he does not go home."

"A good thing too, for the treacherous race to die out in him! Whaι should you care for him? he is your foe."

"I am a Christian," was Richard's answer.

"Well, I promised you whatever you might ask. All my share of his ransom, or his person, bond or free, is yours. You have only to prevail with your own Jarls and bonders."

Richard feared this would be more difficult; but Abbot Martin came to the meeting, and took his part. Moreover, the idea of their hostage dying in their hands, so as to leave them without hold upon the King, had much weight with them; and, after long deliberation, they consented that Lothaire should be restored to his father without ransom, but only on condition that Louis should guarantee to the Duke the peaceable possession of the country as far

16

as St. Clair sur Epte, which had long been in dispute, so that Alberic became, indisputably, a vassal of Normandy.

Perhaps it was the happiest day in Richard's life when he rode back to Bayeux to desire Lothaire to prepare to come with him to St. Clair, there to be given back into the hands of his father.

And there they met King Louis, grave and sorrowful for the loss of his little Carloman, and, for the time, repenting of his misdeeds toward the orphan heir of Normandy.

He pressed the Duke in his arms, and his kiss was a genuine one, as he said, "Duke Richard, we have not deserved this of you. I did not treat you as you have treated my children. We will be true lord and vassal from henceforth."

Lothaire's last words were, "Farewell, Richard. If I lived with you, I might be good like you. I will never forget what you have done for me."

When Richard once more entered Rouen in state, his subjects shouting round him in